D0394167

ANNE & HENRY

ANNE & HENRY

Dawn Ius

Simon Pulse

NEW YORK LONDON TORONTO SYDNEY NEW DELHI

SIMON PULSE

An imprint of Simon & Schuster Children's Publishing Division
1230 Avenue of the Americas, New York, New York 10020
First Simon Pulse hardcover edition September 2015
Text copyright © 2015 by Dawn Ius
Jacket photographs copyright © 2015 by Jill Wachter
All rights reserved, including the right of reproduction in whole or in part in any form.
SIMON PULSE and colophon are registered trademarks of Simon & Schuster, Inc.
For information about special discounts for bulk purchases,
please contact Simon & Schuster Special Sales at 1-866-506-1949
or business@simonandschuster.com.
The Simon & Schuster Speakers Bureau can bring authors to your live event.
For more information or to book an event contact
the Simon & Schuster Speakers Bureau at 1-866-248-3049
or visit our website at www.simonspeakers.com.
Jacket designed by Regina Flath
Interior designed by Hilary Zarycky
The text of this book was set in Berling
Manufactured in the United States of America
2 4 6 8 10 9 7 5 3 1
Ius, Dawn.
Anne & Henry / by Dawn Ius. —First Simon Pulse hardcover edition.
pages cm
Summary: On a rigid path set by his family to become valedictorian, attend
Harvard Law School, have a stunning political career like his father's, and date the
right girl, Henry Tudor feels trapped until he meets the wild, brash Anne Boleyn,
and they embark on a dangerous romance.
ISBN 978-1-4814-3941-1 (hardcover)
[1. Dating (Social customs)—Fiction. 2. Love—Fiction. 3. High schools—Fiction.
4. Schools—Fiction.] I. Title. II. Title: Anne and Henry.
PZ7.1.I97An 2015
[Fic]—dc23
2014046969
ISBN 978-1-4814-3943-5 (ebook)

For Jeffrey
You never let me lose my head when you stole my heart.
I love you.

ANNE & HENRY

CHAPTER ONE
Henry

The Tudor ballroom glitters like we're backstage at a Vegas burlesque. It's too much—the crystal, the diamonds, the people—and there's not nearly enough champagne.

As the music switches to a waltz, I pull Catherine into the middle of the dance floor and begin leading her through the steps, through the crowd of masked faces. Even with years of dance training, it doesn't matter. I always feel out of place at these damn parties.

My girlfriend's spine straightens, her body rigid as she scopes out the room, looking for Medina's most important and influential. She spots our friends dancing toward us and offers a rare smile.

"You look gorgeous, Cath," Liz whispers when she and Wyatt are within earshot. And then to me, "A masquerade ball. Your mom's brilliant, Henry. I feel like a princess."

My father would have hated this—the endless stream of

feathers, gold leaf, and jewels. I hate it too, but my relentless lessons on etiquette rewind, play back at slow speed: "You certainly look like one," I reply with a wink.

"Not one of your better lines," Catherine says under her breath as Liz dances away, giggling, and Wyatt shoots me a glare. Frankly, I'm surprised he's upright—less than twenty minutes ago he and the rest of the guys were smoking up behind the pool house. I don't blame them. If I thought I could get away with it . . .

"Deadly bored, aren't you?" Catherine says. The stem of her diamond-encrusted mask pokes into the side of my rib cage. "You should be proud, Henry. I don't know how your mom did it, but the house looks—"

Gaudy is the word I think she's looking for: A red carpet flows down the middle of our central staircase like a river of blood, a shocking contrast to the usual white that frosts everything from the leather sofas to the marble pillars.

"I'm not looking at the decor," I say, and slide my hands down Catherine's back until they're resting on her ass. The purple gown hugs her hips and her blond hair spills down her shoulders in loose curls. She looks like a fucking queen.

"Don't be inappropriate," she hisses.

"I thought you wanted me to have a good time," I say, and shift my gaze so she doesn't see my grin.

I catch a glimpse of some juniors circling the chocolate

fountain below. One of them pretends to stick his dick in it and the others hoot. I cough out a laugh.

"You *would* find that amusing," Catherine says, her annoyance quickly growing. "How gross."

"Loosen up, Cath," I say, threading my fingers through hers. Jesus, even her skin is cool. I let out a sigh. "Let's go check in with my mother."

At the suggestion, Catherine brightens. "I'll just freshen up first."

"Oh, come on. Why mess with perfection?" My eyebrows rise and fall—twice—and I badly botch a Sean Connery impression. "You're ravishing, darling."

Her mouth forms a line and she tosses my hand aside. "That isn't the slightest bit sexy."

Catherine. Smart and popular, and she *gets* me, or at least the "me" everyone thinks they know. Plus, she's an Aragon, which isn't quite the same as being a Tudor, but since Mom has put herself in charge of finding me an appropriate match in Medina, Catherine tops a very short list.

She kisses my cheek, leaving me stranded in the middle of the dance floor. Another tune kicks in and I scan the crowd for a new partner. Maybe the senator's wife or the assistant principal of Medina Academy, anyone who will take my mind off the mounting tension. I turn to—

My heart catches in my throat.

She is a raven among doves. Bloodred lipstick forms the shape of a heart, striking against her stark black hair and the simple disguise in her hand. Something stirs in my gut.

The girl lowers her mask, and I inhale as though sucker punched. *Those eyes . . .*

She blinks and the trance dissolves. I scrub my hands over my face to readjust my equilibrium and start making my way across the room, pushing through the crowd, trying to maintain eye contact. My face is flushed by the time I get to her, and I thrust my palm out with a jerk.

"Henry," I say. The heart on her lips shifts in an ever-so-slight smirk. I cough out a nervous laugh, and exhaling, add, "I live here."

Jesus Christ. *I live here?* I will the floor to open up and swallow me whole.

Her stare betrays nothing. If only she would just giggle or shake her head, something, anything, to save me from further humiliation. But she remains emotionless, blank.

Almost.

She slides her top teeth over her lower lip, scraping off the bottom half of the heart. Sweat beads at the base of my neck.

"Would you like to dance?" she says.

There's a certain amusement in her voice that puts me on alert. Her eyes crinkle at the edges and I'm sure she's laughing at me. I should back off, but damn it if I don't enjoy a challenge.

I hold out my hand and pull her close. She presses the stem of her mask into my palm—our skin touches. And for one disconcerting moment I've forgotten the steps, lost the ability to dance at all. She reaches up and holds my shoulder as we move across the floor.

My fingers itch to snake through the long tangles of her hair. I focus on the steps instead, the twirls and dips, working hard not to stumble. *Son of a bitch.* I'm all jacked up, my world spinning forward and back, suddenly off-kilter. I can't take my eyes off her haunting face, but even without looking, I know everyone is watching us.

She twirls just out of reach and I yank her back. Whispering in her ear, I say, "Who are you?"

The music stops and a smattering of applause breaks the spell before she can answer. Next thing I know, she's disappearing into the crowd without so much as a backward glance.

I blow out a breath.

Catherine's fingers suddenly intertwine with mine. "And who was *that*?" The slight lift in her voice reveals her jealousy.

I grit my teeth and swallow a knee-jerk response, because I'm pissed off—confused, maybe—by my reaction to *that* girl.

"Henry? Did you hear me?"

"I don't know," I say, letting go of Catherine's hand and loosening the collar of my tuxedo. It's one thing for my girlfriend's insecurities to bubble over at school. Another entirely to make a scene here, where the sheriff's wife stands just a few feet away, ears perked and ready for gossip.

Catherine's eyes dim. "She must be new."

"Seems that way." As a new waltz begins, I make a motion like I want to dance again. But it's not Catherine I'm thinking about as I pull her close, and from the corner of my eye, I spot the girl. She catches me staring and I count the seconds, breaths, heartbeats, before she slowly lifts her disguise.

Fuck me.

As Catherine twirls around, she sees the girl too and freezes midstep. "That's her with your mother and the architect for the creative center," she says. "What's his name? Terry? Travis?"

"Thomas," I mutter, not glancing back. "Thomas Harris."

Catherine clucks her tongue. "She's a bit . . . harsh looking, don't you think?"

The comment is classic Catherine. Classic Medina, I guess. The whole damn town is crammed onto a tiny pedestal, pushing and shoving, jockeying for position as they claw their way to the top.

"I guess we should introduce ourselves," I say.

Catherine fakes a smile. "Of course. But only for a minute, right?" She rubs her hand along my biceps and squeezes. "Charles and Marie are sneaking a bottle of champagne out to the dock. I promised we'd join them." She drops her voice to a whisper. "I can't wait to slip out of these shoes—they're killing me."

Catherine's long gown hides five-inch heels, an effort to disguise her height. At six-foot-two, I tower over her. "Trust me, a million other places I'd rather be too."

Which is turning out to be a bold-faced lie.

The closer we get to the girl, the louder my mother's cackle echoes over the white noise of laughter, small talk, and music. Life without Dad and my brother hasn't been easy for her the past year—hell, it hasn't been easy for either of us. But somehow she's managed to rise from the ashes of grief like a fiery phoenix, this evening's gala the final step to full-on resurrection. Me? I'm still buried under the wreckage.

Catherine hangs on to me. This new girl has shoved her right out of her comfort zone. I feel guilty about it—because even though I shouldn't be staring, I am.

What's left of the painted heart on the girl's lips cracks on our approach, revealing a small gap between her teeth.

"Hello again," I say, warmth spreading across my cheeks.

She nods, stares. My face goes hot and I'm at a loss for words.

Catherine's fingers move from my elbow to my shoulder, and tighten with a possessive squeeze. She crooks her neck, leans into me, and her blond hair spills over my tux.

"I don't know what's gotten into my boyfriend tonight.

Must be the alcohol in the punch." She smiles, but even from my view it looks more like a sneer. "I'm Catherine."

The girl's lips part and I catch a flash of something silver in her mouth. My throat dries to sandpaper. Is that a tongue piercing? Jesus. Everything about this girl is sexy as hell.

Catherine clears her throat, squeezes too tight. "And you are?"

"Anne." The girl smiles a little. "Anne Boleyn."

CHAPTER TWO

Anne

I can't help but stare as Henry shifts awkwardly at his Barbie girlfriend's obvious unease. He seems cocky and pretentious. Really not my type.

I've got eyes, though.

"You just moved here?" Barbie says, flashing me another make-believe smile. Fitting, since this whole mansion looks like it belongs in a fairy tale.

"Oh good, you've all met," Mrs. Tudor's voice coos before I can bite off a sarcastic response. She lowers her ruby-lined mask and rests a hand on her son's forearm. "Come, Henry. Mr. Harris has the plans for the new center with him. You'll want to take a look." She leans forward and, to me, adds, "Your father is so talented."

"Stepfather," I correct.

Her smile falters only a second. "Of course. My apologies. We're just so thrilled to have the country's most celebrated architect here at our gala." I resist the urge to roll my eyes.

Mrs. Tudor leads her son away, her head bent toward his ear in a hushed whisper. Lagging behind, I can't make out all the words—something about my mother being a former waitress—but I can read between the lines.

Bitch.

Henry shakes my stepfather's hand. "I've seen your preliminary work, sir," he says, all gushing and cute. "It's impressive. I wish I could perform on that stage. I know my way around the old theater."

My skin prickles a little at the lame admission and I study Henry's build, the way his tux shows off his broad chest, lean legs. No doubt about it, the guy's got a great ass. But an actor? I don't see it.

"Art is a skill best practiced," my stepfather says, and this time, I do roll my eyes. "What are your plans next year? We could use some experienced help when things get up and running."

"Henry has applied to Harvard," Mrs. Tudor says, a little too quickly.

My mother swoops in from the sidelines, her smile of approval all glittery. "A business tycoon in the making?"

"He'll be senator one day," Mrs. Tudor says. She's in her element now, obviously well versed in the role of political cheerleader. "My late husband passed his acumen on to his sons. Henry has already started his career."

"Interesting," I say, though I'm bored as shit. "So, you're on Student Council or something?"

Henry stands taller, proud, poised to impress, his chest puffed out like he's solved world poverty. "President, actually. Have a question for council?"

Mischief tugs at the corners of my lips. "I heard I can't park my motorcycle on school property. Afraid it might clash with your precious Jaguar?"

Henry's eyes twinkle. "Audi."

"That's enough, Anne," my stepfather growls.

"I'm sure you'll agree with the rule when you see the school grounds, dear," Mrs. Tudor says. "They're quite stunning." She glances back at Barbie, who adds, "You get a great view of Lake Washington from almost every classroom. It's a beautiful place for prom. Are you a senior, Anne?"

"Junior," I say. Not like she cares.

"Perfect. You'll have two years to get used to the place before graduation." She offers me a coy sneer so subtle no one else would notice. "Maybe even fall in love. Find your own Prince Charming."

I almost laugh aloud.

"Forgive me if I'm being presumptuous," my stepfather says, oblivious to the tension, the message Barbie is sending. He drapes his arm around my shoulder and I tense up. "I really want Anne and her mother to fit in here. Would you be willing to give her a tour of the school? Maybe pick her up tomorrow on her first day and show her the way?"

My stomach clenches. Is he kidding?

"Oh, I couldn't." Barbie presses her hand against her chest. "I mean, I'd love to, of course. But I have cheerleading practice tomorrow." She seems to regain her composure, as though she's just dodged an unwieldy arrow. "I'm the squad leader."

Of course.

There's a beat of awkward silence, a slight hesitation in time, and then—

"I'll do it." Henry's Adam's apple bobs. "Give me your address. I'll pick you up at seven."

My stomach clamps like I've been drop-kicked, and the chill of Barbie's gaze is enough to give me frostbite. "Don't you have football practice, Henry?" she says through clenched teeth. And then to me whispers, "He's the quarterback."

All so very cliché.

"Afternoon practice," Henry says.

Based on the slight slur in his voice, I'm not sure he's up to play morning tour guide, but I keep my mouth shut. Frankly, I'm shocked they're serving drinks to minors, even if it is just champagne. Maybe Medina isn't as prissy as I thought.

My stepfather pats Henry on the arm, my mother breathes some kind of thank-you, and while they slide into easy banter about the Seahawks and politics, my pained silence stretches into eternity.

"We should get back to our friends," Barbie says, looping her gloved hand through Henry's arm, steering him away from me, clinging to some kind of fairy tale romance.

Yeah, I believed in it once, too.

My mother makes nice with Mrs. Tudor, bending her head forward to whisper and compliment, to tell tall tales. It's like she already thinks she belongs here, fits right in. She doesn't.

Neither of us do.

My new world is etched in diamonds and sealed in gold, drowning in pretension. With each insignificant hour that I spend here, my dreadful past blurs and fades.

Disappears.

With any luck, soon I won't remember it at all.

A thread of resentment coils around my neck. Thomas may have saved us from poverty and shame, but the rescue comes with expectations. How am I supposed to blend in with all of—

This?

A masked waiter hands me a champagne flute. I sip, roll it around with my tongue. Swallow. Repeat. I'd kill for something stronger. "I'll be at the buffet if anyone needs me," I say, my eyes on the volcano erupting with chocolate lava.

Before I can escape, Mrs. Tudor says, "Your mother tells me you've had a rough past. It's a shame Henry and Catherine didn't take time to introduce you to some of their friends."

Her eyes glisten with the illusion of sincerity. She sizes up my dress, the curve of flesh that rises from the low-cut bodice. "Feel free to mingle. I'm sure you won't have any trouble getting around."

Fuck her.

I swallow the last of the liquid in one gulp, but the lump of unease in my throat doesn't move. It grows and swells, daring me to say something in my own defense.

Thomas has made it clear that this party, these people, are important.

I ease away from Mrs. Tudor, my mother, and the suffocating expectation of putting on a good show.

Four guys about my age stand at the end of the dining table, laughing, talking, raising their flutes in raucous cheer. I consider saying hi, getting the tough stuff out of the way— I've never been great at introductions. But Mrs. Tudor's voice echoes in my ear and I hesitate. I pull up the top of my dress, cover a bit of skin, mask cleavage, and hover behind the chocolate fountain, just out of sight. Sudden insecurity sinks its teeth in, vicious and biting.

Why the hell am I already letting these people get to me?

A male voice rises over the white noise of chatter, obnoxious, maybe drunk. "Hey John, did you check out the new chick?"

Are they talking about me? I peer around the fountain. Another voice, less obnoxious, less drunk: "I heard her mother is shacked up with the architect."

"Just another gold digger, then."

The thump in my chest fades to a dull ache. My ears prick up anxiously. I hear them all the way at the end of the table—the whole room probably can.

"She looks like she's got a chip on her shoulder," another says, and I wonder if he's John.

"Sounds perfect. John loves a ball breaker."

I suck back a gasp. I should walk away, go far away.

"Seriously, you assholes obviously don't know shit about me," the guy says, and I'm sure this is John. I sneak a glance. His muscular body and sharp cheekbones are torn from the pages of a magazine. Broad shoulders, tapered torso, strong legs. He's probably a jock; he looks like a jock.

I'm so not into jocks.

"Come on, you wouldn't tap that?"

Unease creeps through every inch of my body. I stare past the fountain into the glamorous crowd, and blink, blink, blink.

John scoffs. And suddenly he's not handsome at all, more sleazy tabloid than GQ. "She looks like a skank," he says. "I like a bit of a challenge, you know?"

A chorus of laughs, and then from the obnoxious guy: "I'll bet my Porsche you can't get into her pants by Thanksgiving."

I tune out the echo of voices, their words. Embarrassment builds into something dangerous. Humiliation spreads up my neck.

STOP.

I close my eyes and Mrs. Tudor's sneer fills the darkness. *I'm sure you won't have trouble getting around.* Fuck her. Fuck John. Screw all of them and their pretentious judgment. I won't let these people, my past, my guilt control me. And before I can think it over, consider the consequences, I'm strutting—strutting!—toward the four of them, toward John, a chocolate-dipped strawberry in my hand.

The room fades around me, the glitter, the shimmer, all of it just disappears. It's me—

And them.

The boys quiet on my approach, mouths open in slight shock. I don't blame them, I'm shocked too. But there's something about being in control that makes me feel *alive.*

I bite into the strawberry, allowing the juices to wet my dry mouth and soothe the scratch in my throat. My gaze narrows in on John and I bite, suck, chew, swallow.

John's face pales, goes so white I can see into him, *through* him. And even though I shouldn't, I like it. The attention, the way John looks at me, as if he wants me.

"Impressive," I say, intentionally leaving it vague.

John rubs one hand behind his neck. "Yeah, Henry's mom knows how to throw a party, that's for sure." He pauses, and then, "You must be the new girl."

"Your powers of deduction astound me," I say.

There's a collective "oooh" from his friends. I gaze at him with round eyes.

John falters a bit, but recovers quickly—definitely a jock; I *hate* jocks—and puffs out his chest, making the first move. Playing right into my hands.

He gives me a wolfish leer, like he's a pro at this whole devilishly charming gig. "You look like a troublemaker," he says.

I throw back my head and laugh, one of those ridiculous bimbo laughs, the kind that makes me sick, makes me lose faith in women a little. "Guilty," I say with a shrug, then lean in close. My lips hover over John's neck, raise the tiny hairs on his skin. The energy radiating from his body tingles on my mouth.

"You wanna make some trouble together?" The throaty purr sounds foreign, not like me at all.

I pull back, scan John's face. His gaze darts from my eyes to my lips, searching for truth, lies. He settles on my mouth. I flick my tongue ever so slightly. Seconds pass in slow motion. I don't move, not one

damned

muscle.

"You've, uh, got a little chocolate on the corner of your mouth," John says. He's flirting now, showing how he can play me, how it will be so *easy* to get into my pants.

I exhale slowly, a silent cue for him to make the next move.

Come on.

John's eyes are hazy, dull. His face goes ashen, almost gray with wanting—

He leans forward. Wets his lips. Moves in so close I can smell the booze on this breath. "It looks tasty," he says.

My response is another soft purr. An invitation.

John's face hovers over mine, invading my space. It takes every effort to control my muscles, to keep my lips from spasming into a full twitch, a soft snicker.

"I want to lick your mouth clean," he says, sounding sexy. Or trying.

His lips are almost on mine now, partially open. He inches closer, closing in on his prize.

I wipe away the chocolate and suck on my finger. As I pull back, the gap between us widens. "Mmmm . . . divine."

John's expression falters, but he doesn't give up. "You want sweet? I'm right here, baby."

I bark out a laugh. "Not even if you were the last asshole on the planet."

This time I've got him.

Heat creeps up his neck. His face blossoms in full red, and I know—know without question—that he is humiliated, embarrassed. And mad.

Shit, he's mad.

I turn on my heel and walk past his shocked friends, past the fountain, past the crowd. I am focused, empowered, a little bit giddy when I look up.

My heart slams into my throat.

Henry stands at the second floor railing, staring down at me, at the scene, at everything that has just happened. A shiver runs all the way up my spine, turns me inside out.

Our eyes connect.

And just when I think I've made a mistake, wonder if I've screwed up horribly, sealed my fate in this town, Henry lifts his champagne glass in salute.

CHAPTER THREE
Henry

Anne's skirt rises and her pale thigh presses against the black seat cushion of my Audi. Damn, I wish those legs weren't so completely bare. *Eyes on the road, Henry.*

Truth is, I haven't stopped thinking about Anne since last night. I can't shake the image of her heart-shaped lips, those hypnotic eyes. I've never seen passion like that before, never in eyes so haunting and beautiful.

Meanwhile, Anne stares straight out the window, like she's memorizing every inch of the landscape: the rising sun skulking just behind the mountain, creating the illusion that it's on fire; the massive trees that line the asphalt, gray against the inky depths of Lake Washington.

I know every nuance of this particular road—the sharp hairpin curve at the quarter mile, the upcoming lookout point, the long straightaway that begs to be driven hard.

Every skid mark, a story: dodging raccoons, learning to drive with Arthur, street racing with the guys. My adrenaline pulses with the need to go fast, but as Anne and I hit the home-stretch, instead of stepping on the gas, I ease off. Drag out our time together.

"Maybe you're not taking me to the school at all," Anne says with a hint of amusement.

I steal a sideways glance at her. Those thigh-high boots are a total uniform violation, but fuck me if they aren't scorching. I shift in my seat.

"Busted," I say. "I'm actually kidnapping you and dragging you off to my secret serial killer cabin in the woods. Every-thing you know about me is a lie." I widen my eyes in mock horror. "My name's not even Henry."

She wags her cell phone at me, pretending to look seri-ous. "I've got Medina PD on auto-dial, you know."

My grin widens. It should be awkward—we're yin and yang—but instead being with Anne feels surprisingly . . . freeing.

Her sharp gasp turns my attention back to the road as the ominous shadow of Medina Academy looms into view. "It's a fucking fortress," she says. Anne leans forward and puts both hands on the dash for a closer look, her shirt lifting a little to reveal a thin band of peach skin on her lower back. I grip the steering wheel so tight my knuckles go white.

"All that's missing is the moat," I say with a sarcastic drawl.

"I bet the view from the top floor is killer."

My gaze flits to Anne's face, to those amazing eyes, now as big as soccer balls. I chuckle, shift down, and cruise into the parking lot. I park close to the main entrance in the spot marked with my name. I get the sense Anne isn't easy to impress, and my pulse spikes with the sharp thrill of the chase.

Anne cranes her neck, looks up, way up to the caps of the turrets on either side of the school's front entrance. An enormous flag hangs between the stone pillars, all red, white, blue, and proud.

"Fancy," Anne says, and pops open the passenger door. "My motorcycle really wouldn't fit in." She steps onto the asphalt and stretches, reaching her arms high over her head. I climb out of the car and rest my hip on the bumper, waiting for her to take it all in. I pretend I'm not staring at the smooth flesh of her exposed lower stomach. She glances back and smirks. Busted again.

"These boots are over the top, aren't they?" she says.

I scan the length of them, the crisscross lacing that extends almost to her knees, and a whimper catches in my windpipe. "Fitting in is overrated."

There's a skip of hesitation, as though she's concerned, worried maybe, about exactly that: fitting in. A little shy, nervous, insecure. It's not the impression I have of her at all.

As we walk to the entrance, she checks out the landscaping—

the meticulous diagonal lines in the grass, the polished stones in the red rock sidewalk, flowers crammed everywhere. I've seen the books; Medina Academy spends a pretty penny on maintenance. And the awestruck look on Anne's face almost makes it worth it.

"Who's the groundskeeper, Martha Stewart?" she says.

I bark out a laugh and hold the door as she enters. She slides by and our shoulders touch, sending a shockwave down my spine.

"We'll hit the office later," I manage without stuttering, then point down the hallway cluttered with cautionary tape. "And we'll steer clear of the west wing. Renovations."

Anne trails her fingers along the stone walls as we walk. Her heels *click*, *clack*, echo on the marble floor.

"The original structure is too heavy for the soil or something, and has to be rebuilt." I pause, grind my lower jaw. I'm boring the hell out of her. "I guess since your stepdad's an architect, you'd know more about this stuff."

"I don't give a shit about architecture."

My voice lowers. "Administration has strict guidelines about swearing, Miss Boleyn." She's clearly amused and I know I should shut up, quit while I'm ahead. I don't. "One of the many rules my brother enforced as student president."

They're part of the ironclad Code of Conduct that Arthur cowrote, giving students the power to reprimand or expel peers who don't fit the Medina mold. A mock courtroom was even created for trials.

Anne smiles, her face expectant and playful. I could get whiplash trying to keep up with her emotions. "Real life of the party, huh?" She spins around to face me, walks backward, her cherry-colored lips pursed and teasing. "Following in big brother's footsteps doesn't sound like much fun."

Her flippant comment makes me flinch. It's clear she doesn't know that Arthur's dead.

On the second floor, we pause outside the music room and peer in. Dozens of instruments hang from the walls like high-end art, more aesthetic than functional. Medina Academy hasn't won any band awards as far back as I can remember, but the music department spends enough to feed the deception.

Anne lingers at the door, scoping out the drum kit, the trombone, a handful of guitars. A white piano takes up an entire corner of the room, its dusty ivory keys yellowed under the fluorescent light. Catherine used to play. But in tenth grade, she traded in her piano teacher for Coach Fuller and music took a backseat to cheerleading, the only time she's ever stood up to her parents about anything. The thought of Catherine pokes at me, a sharp intrusion of guilt. I refocus on Anne.

"Do you play an instrument?" I say.

"Sax," she says.

I choke on air. "Excuse me?"

Anne grins. "I play the saxophone."

A nervous chuckle escapes my lips, twists into embarrassed heat. "Seriously? That's cool."

Anne punches my shoulder, lightly, but my whole body responds to her touch. "Do I look like I play the sax?"

I frown, confused. "So you don't?"

Her hypnotic black eyes lighten, flicker with mischief. She's totally playing me. I'm so not used to getting played. "Why sax?"

"Because it's the last thing you expected me to say."

She's right. Nothing about Anne is what I expect.

We pass the art room and studio, spend a few minutes in the library. Anne touches the spines of old novels as though they might crack, pauses at a random book. She flips open *Le Deuxième Sexe*, reads the first page, her lips moving in slow motion. I try not to think about the title, the stark black-and-white cover. The way her mouth looks when she reads aloud.

Anne slides the book back in place. "de Beauvoir is a genius."

"Absolutely," I say, twisting the little white lie until it becomes truth. I've never read the book in Anne's hand, not one single page, but like hell I'll admit it.

We move from the library to a Student Council office down the hall. It's crammed with solid oak and polished brass, more law office than high school hang-out, formal and stuffy. Two leather chairs frame a glass coffee table.

Arthur's spirit lingers here, practically suffocating.

I keep hoping that it will get easier, that the pain will fade and I'll stop thinking about my brother every day. How it should have been me who went off that cliff last spring. How if I hadn't bailed, I could have saved him.

Anne and I pause at the grid of photographs on the back wall, framed pictures of successful politicians, athletes, Arthur. So much Arthur. More than a dozen stills, various poses and expressions.

She zeroes in on an older picture of my brother and Principal Adams, just minutes after signing the school's Code of Conduct, chins high and proud, like they're passing the First Amendment.

I want to take this photograph down, box it up with the rest of his things, bury them in the basement, *under* the basement, along with my guilt. "That's Arthur."

"You look like him," Anne says. She leans in for a closer view, her emotions blank and unreadable.

My face reflects in the glass picture frame, milky and unfocused, a reminder that while our features are similar, I'll never be Arthur, will never quite measure up. The black hole in my chest widens. "He's dead," I say, maybe for shock.

"I'm sorry," Anne whispers, her gaze skimming from one image to the next.

"This isn't a photo collage, it's a shrine," she says, and I'm surprised she notices. She pauses on another photo, squinting as though to find a familiar face in the crowd. When she cocks her head, I know she spots Catherine. I can almost hear the clunk of gears shifting in her brain as she studies the way Arthur and my girlfriend are posed—interlinked hands, bodies slanted toward each other, lovestruck expressions projecting the kind of happiness I'm convinced only happens in movies.

She gives me a quizzical look.

I offer a terse nod, gnaw on my lower lip. "It's complicated."

It's not, actually. As the lone children from the two most influential families in Medina, our relationship was encouraged, expected even, after Arthur's death. With both my father and brother gone, I've inherited it all—the grief, the drama, the responsibility. Catherine. I'm a follower. Picking up where my brother left off. Living another man's life. Maybe not by choice, but it doesn't make it any less true.

I'm relieved when Anne presses forward.

"Was he a good president?" she says.

The question catches me off guard. He wasn't a *good* president, he was *the* president, leaving behind footsteps so large and overwhelming not even a giant could fill them. "Only the best," I say.

Anne smiles sadly. "What happened to him?"

I shake my head to show discomfort. She gets it and

suddenly I'm anxious to leave this room. I glance at the clock above the cherrywood desk. My brother's. Drawers overflow with his personal things—business cards, election pins, documents, an autographed Seahawks pennant.

"We should go. Class starts soon," I say.

Anne nods, but she lingers at my brother's desk and lifts the only framed picture of me in the room—a group shot of the current council members. "Just one girl in the bunch," Anne remarks, not with judgment, but awareness.

"Yeah, that's Samantha. Sam," I say, without looking. "She's the council secretary."

Anne shoots me an annoyed look and I shrug.

"Hey, I don't control the voting."

On our way to the courtyard we pass the gym and pause at the trophy case filled with statues, medals, certificates. My name is engraved on more than half. I glance at Anne through my peripheral vision, looking for signs she's impressed. It's suddenly so damn important that she's impressed. I want her to see me for *me*, not the shadow of my brother.

"Quite an amazing collection of trophies," she says. "Football quarterback, tennis, captain of the rowing team—tell me Superman, where *do* you keep your cape?"

"It's at the dry cleaner's at the moment," I say, and she snorts.

Students mill all around us, gearing up for first period. These sprawling courtyard gardens are a labyrinth of dense greenery dotted with park benches and tables—the place to gather, study. Make out.

I want to take Anne somewhere private, spend a few minutes getting to know her better. But there's no escaping the yahoos strolling toward us: Charles, Rick, and John. Anne sees them too. The air around us, around Anne, frosts with tension. I hold my chin high. One false move and my friends will know that something's off, that maybe I dig Anne a little more than I should.

"I believe you've already met the jesters," I say to Anne. I slap Charles on the back, nod at Rick, cast a warning glance at John. He's had an entire night to recover and plot some type of revenge for his humiliation.

"Don't let Henry fool you," Rick says. "He's the prankster here."

Anne shifts and bites her sexy lower lip. She tilts her head a little, then says to John, her voice dripping with sarcasm, "I think we all know who the real joke is."

Church bells ring, signaling the start of class.

CHAPTER FOUR
Anne

I walk into chem, compose my face, and prepare for the worst. The awkward school introductions, the questioning stares, the fake kindness. I shrug off my backpack, the lingering sense of unease after seeing John—he's such a jerk—and plop onto a stool at the only empty workstation in the back of the room, avoiding eye contact.

The class is small, around a dozen, two to a desk.

A handful of students whisper about boys, cars, the principal's unibrow. It's the chitchat gossip of familiarity, of kids who've grown up together, hung out together, passed, failed, skipped together.

I hate being the new girl.

A door swings open and the teacher enters, leading with a big, easy grin and a shopping cart of pumpkins. Tall, squat, fat—six of them in various shades of orange.

I pull myself into proper sitting position, intrigued, a little confused. Flipping open my textbook and schedule, I double check that I'm in the right room.

"Greetings, minions," the teacher says. He parks the cart at the front of the class, slides out of his sports jacket and into a white lab coat, a cheesy smile stretched wide across his face. He points it at me like it's a loaded weapon and fires off a welcoming shot. "You must be Anne. I'm Peter Galvin. I'll answer to almost anything, though." A quick pause. "Except Pete. My mother calls me Pete."

The room fills with laughter. It's loud and false and makes me wince. The class has heard all of these jokes before. I slump low on my stool, rest my elbows on the desk, rub hard on the inside of my left wrist.

Galvin pushes his glasses up the bridge of his nose with one finger, then scrubs his hands together like he's making a fire, eyes wide, impossible grin growing wider and wider until—

"Kaboom!" He explodes with enthusiasm. "We're going to have a blast today, kids."

I cock one eyebrow. Maybe I expected someone a little stuffier?

"So I bet you're all wondering what's up," he says.

He rolls the shopping cart around the room, placing a pumpkin at each workstation. The tall desks form a semi-circle facing the front of the class. Side tables overflow with beakers, Bunsen burners, various implements of chemistry.

A banner stenciled with the periodic table stretches across the back wall. "In honor of the season, I've scared up a frighteningly good experiment." The class groans. Pumpkins and puns.

What a geek.

The proud look on Galvin's face is brilliant and I'm caught up in his thrill. He almost makes it easy to forget I'm the new girl.

Until I realize this is a group assignment and I'll be paired off. My throat constricts. There's an odd number of students, an extra. Me.

"Since we seem to have a missing student this morning," Galvin says, freezing me with one of those easy grins, "you can work with me, Anne." He plants a stalky pumpkin on the desk. "I'll be right there. The rest of you—"

Galvin's gaze shifts to the opening classroom door and flashes with annoyance.

"Mr. Thompson, how nice of you to grace us with your presence." He glances down at his watch. "And only a few minutes past the hour. Please, share with us your excuse this time."

"Sorry, teach. I was chatting up the ladies and missed the bell."

Snickering ripples through the class. My insides twist. I already know that voice. It grates on the back of my skull and turns my veins cold.

John.

"Illuminating," Galvin says. "Given your mad skills with the ladies, I'm sure you won't mind working with your new classmate, then. I'd like you to meet—"

"We've met," I say. It's clear now I should have left John alone at the party, kept away from him and his friends. Let them believe the worst of me. Like I'm not already used to that.

If Galvin hears the tension or senses John's disgust, he ignores it and refocuses on the class.

John slithers across the room, finds me hiding in the back, spreading newspaper on the workstation, gathering a small knife, a glass dish. I've been in Medina a couple of days and I've already had enough of John.

"Together again," he says.

I bite back a sarcastic response and slide into my lab coat.

Galvin writes on a whiteboard at the front of the class in orange and black. "Your first task is to carve a pumpkin," he says. He draws a simple jack-o'-lantern face, triangular eyes, nose, a long mouth with three teeth, two up, one down. "Now, for all of you Picassos in the room, you'll need to keep your pumpkin faces simple." He taps on the picture, pokes his finger through one hand-drawn eye. "This is about as artistic as I want you to get."

A student on the opposite side of the room snickers, raises his voice. "No fair. I've already drawn my Frankenstein face."

"You *are* a Frankenstein face," a girl chimes in.

I recognize her as one of Catherine's friends, a sparkly princess from the party.

John yanks our pumpkin toward him, slides the knife in and out of its flesh in a circle around the stem. "Sorry to wreck your daydream, darling, but this class doesn't go all day." He pulls the top off and the pumpkin's guts hang like human entrails, ragged and slimy.

"Go ahead, get right in there," John says, nudging his head toward the cavernous hole in the top of the gourd. "You seem the type that likes to get dirty."

I snort. Stick my hands in the pumpkin and pull out a handful of guts and squish them around, fold them over my knuckles. A long, stringy strand slides between my fingers and lands on the newspaper with a gushy splat. I drop the rest of the guts on top, poking around for seeds to separate them from the pile of slimy orange mush. It seeps under my fingernails, taints my chipped black polish.

"What is this? Food studies? Just get the shit out of there," John says, more growl than command.

I flutter my lashes, thrilled I've gotten under his skin. "You wish I was kneading you like this."

John's wolf grin deepens. "A little culinary foreplay? Now that's hot."

I choke on a laugh, for once unable to offer a comeback.

He wipes the pumpkin's skin clean with a paper towel, scrawls out a simple face with a black Sharpie. One eye is bigger than the other, the nose too small. I swallow the urge to say something—it is cute in a dysfunctional sort of way. I snatch up the knife and wait for John to pass over the pumpkin.

"You think I'm letting you anywhere near me with a sharp object?" His mouth twists into a sneer.

Galvin paces the room, inspecting our faces. "Make sure you cut all the way through," he says, and mimes a sawing motion with his hand. "You want the pieces to slide in and out easily."

At the class's combined chortling, he holds up his palm. "*Mature*, people. Real mature."

I focus on John's steady hand, the small tufts of dark hair on his knuckles, the way his tongue sticks out from the corner of his mouth as he concentrates on the task. The first pumpkin segment drops out, lands on the newsprint. I wipe it clean, wait, repeat.

John's cheeks puff out. He cuts one tooth at a time.

"Think we could speed it up?" I say.

He looks up. His dark eyes are full of misgivings and mischief. "Maybe I like to go slow."

"I heard you were more of a two-minute guy."

His mouth twitches, like he can't decide whether to chuckle or sneer, as though doing either would concede a point in my favor. "Stop living in the past," he finally says, unaware of how deep those wounds cut. "You've been playing with boys until now. Real men live in Medina, babe."

"Yeah?" I say, raising an eyebrow. "Maybe you could point one out when you see him."

Galvin pauses at our station, squints at the pumpkin. "One eye is lopsided," he says, and drops a sparkler, plus seven pea-size gray pebbles on the newsprint. They smell like the inside of fireworks, a little like rotting eggs. "There are earplugs in the cupboard. Consider wearing them when we do the experiment."

"Sounds good to me," John mutters.

Galvin returns to the front of the class, clears his throat. "In 1862, Friedrich Wöhler discovered that calcium carbide and water would react to form a very flammable gas." He scrawls a formula on the board, adds orange flames and a sad face emoticon. "We're going to demonstrate that reaction with our jack-o'-lanterns."

My skin tingles with curiosity.

"Now, slide the pumpkin segments back into place—the face should be intact, like you haven't carved anything," Galvin says. "Then, turn your masterpiece around so it faces the center of the room."

John pushes in the eyes, the nose, struggles a bit with the mouth. I shave a little flesh from the pumpkin's mug and his teeth glide into place. "We just needed to loosen it up a bit," I say.

He guffaws, covers his mouth with his hand. "I guess you'd know about being loose."

Here, I could crush him, but I bite my lower lip, refusing to take the bait. It's my first day, and people are already watching me, trying to figure me out. How much of *me* do I want to put on display? I've been there before, fucked up, barely recovered.

"Poke a small hole through the back of your pumpkin," Galvin says, pausing after each instruction to ensure everyone keeps up. "And then pour a small layer of peroxide at the bottom of the gourd."

As soon as I do, it begins to react with the pumpkin, starts to gurgle and froth, dissolving the skin like some kind of flesh-eating disease. John pours water into an empty tuna can, sets it in the bottom of the pumpkin, and adds the calcium carbide pebbles.

"We've only got a few minutes here, guys, so here's what's going to happen," Galvin says. His voice rises, enthusiasm taking hold. The room buzzes with infectious anticipation.

"Insert your sparkler into the hole at the back of your pumpkin." Galvin moves over to the light switch, pauses. "I'm going to turn off the lights. Count to ten—that shouldn't be too hard, right?" He carries on despite the groans. "On ten, light the sparkler. But"—he holds up a finger. Holy shit, I can hardly wait. "Don't forget to put the lid on. I want one of you to keep your hand on the top. Make sure you're wearing your oven mitt."

John tosses the red potholder at me, scowls. "That's your job. You wouldn't catch me dead with one of those on."

I'm too excited to respond, to think of a snide remark. I press my gloved hand down against the stem. My heart races, threatens to pop, pop—

Click.

The room goes dark. My senses are on high alert. The scent of sulfur lingers in the air and my skin tingles. John's breath is hot on my neck. "You wanna make some trouble together?"

The teasing edge of his voice is replaced by something ravenous and exposed. It's not just that I've wounded his pride. There's something more, and this class, this moment, isn't going to even the score. I try not to think about it, not here, not now.

Just get through the day. The week. This whole damn year.

Lighters flick in unison.

John lights our sparkler. It fizzes and sizzles, creating a small fireworks display. I push back the stinging memories of the past and forget about John, his ego, forget everything but this. Hold my breath, wait for something to happen, for the chemical reaction to—

Bang!

Pumpkin eyes, noses, teeth explode into the air and six orange bursts of light flash in the darkness. For a split second, a half-dozen gourds grin at me, say hello, glow in welcome, before they simply blink out.

It worked. I can hardly believe it. Can barely keep my smile from taking over my whole damn face.

"Kaboom," John whispers, his mouth right against my ear, and my stomach drops down, all the way down to the floor, lands *under* the floor. "Who knew we'd have such explosive chemistry?"

CHAPTER FIVE

Henry

Here's how this night should go.

I'll throw on another tuxedo and head over to the mayor's house. I'll nod and make polite, intelligent conversation about health care, women's rights, and immigration. I'll debate gun laws and listen to how I look *just* like my dead brother and how my father, rest his soul, is missed and revered.

Touching, right? Except I know politicians are the best bullshitters in the business.

My father, his father, and even my great-grandfather believed in action above promise, in making life better for the people they represented. We founded this town, but under the surface of each practiced VIP's smile, their envy festers. Medina is full of people just waiting for me to fuck up—for another family name to waltz in and take center stage.

I fidget with my bowtie, adjusting it so it rests dead center on my freshly pressed shirt. I catch my reflection in the mirror, the tired circles under my eyes. Football, rowing, homework, event after event. I look like a damn corpse.

My mother hovers behind me, the mirror skewing her taller and thinner. Her royal blue dress clings to her and diamonds hang from her neck and ears. *The Tudor matriarch.* Most days, like today, she can pretend that she's okay, that everything will be fine. We both know it won't be.

"You look just like him, you know," she says with a soft, sad sigh. I don't know if she means Arthur or Dad, maybe both. Disappointment has burrowed deep into her bones, leaving her weak and vulnerable.

Under my mother's body armor, she's a shell of the woman she used to be, and when she snaps, it'll be my fault. That fear is what powers me through the darkness, searching for the light on the other side, and gives me the strength to pretend that *this* is what I want.

"Arthur would have known how to wear these," I say, holding up my wrists to reveal the unclasped white-gold cufflinks engraved with my initials. "Maybe I should wear his instead."

It's a bit tongue in cheek, a test to see if she'll bite.

"Tonight is all about you, Henry."

Tonight is definitely *not* all about me. My mother relies on these events to gain the ear of the mayor and other local politicians, an opportunity to schmooze, secure her place in the limelight. I've never understood why it's so important to her. Or why it's supposed to be for me. Wouldn't it be better, easier even, to stop pretending to be something we're not? To let someone else take over?

She crosses the room and fastens the cufflinks with cool, capable fingers. I blink as if to take a snapshot, freeze this moment in time. This is the most intimate thing she's done in the year since my dad died of cardiac arrest.

"You know I want what's best for you," she says. "It's what your father wanted too." Sincerity glints in her eyes and I'm desperate to believe her. "The limo awaits," she adds, quickly returning to the curt tone I'm used to.

I nod, masking my lackluster enthusiasm with a fake smile. I'm well-versed in little white lies, have practiced them ever since my father died and left behind his ridiculous list of conditions and rules: go to an Ivy League school, immerse myself in politics, marry a Tudor-approved girl—or forget my inheritance.

I consider calling Catherine and bribing her to join me. She's often the voice of reason at these stuffy functions, the youth in a room full of old men in overpriced suits and the lingering scent of exotic cigars. I get a kick out of watching her work a room.

I send Catherine a quick text instead: *Wish me luck.*

Her response is immediate. *You're a Tudor. You don't need it. Tell my dad he looks handsome—new suit!*

Catherine's father is Senator Davis's campaign manager. It's how I'm supposed to get my "in"—an internship with him after college.

Thanks for the heads-up, I reply.

When we're in the limo, my mother sips champagne and crams my brain with facts and statistics. She quizzes and tests, repeats, explains. I stretch out on the leather seat cushion and stare at the velvet ceiling.

"What is your stance on gun control?" she says.

Shoot me now.

I press my lips together and blink hard. Erase the images etched into my brain, trying to focus and clear away thoughts of Catherine, Anne. Especially Anne. Jesus, why am I even thinking about Anne?

The mayor's house is tucked into a cove of evergreen trees, a red rock manor overlooking the lake. Our limo pulls up to the curb and idles while I step onto the sidewalk and wrap a shawl around my mother's shoulders. She takes my arm and we cross a cobblestone bridge, aim for the front entrance—a solid oak door framed by stone pillars. Chinese paper lanterns line a path to the left of us, leading to a giant patio. Tonight, the water fountain will flicker in red, white, and blue in honor of the evening's political agenda.

The mayor's wife opens the door and greets my mother with a quick peck and me with an extended hug. I have a soft spot for Susan Mandell. She's always been able to find me—the *real* me—in a crowded room of political piranhas. She might be the only one who doesn't compare me to my brother. "You look handsome," she says, and plants a wet kiss on my cheek.

I spot all of the usual suspects stuffed into tuxedos like penguins, milling about the room, pecking at appetizers, funneling booze. Catherine's father sees me and nods. We'll spend half an hour networking and BS-ing before Senator Davis addresses the room to unveil his presidential campaign strategy. That's where I'm expected to pounce, offer abiding support, commit to him and his causes.

"Henry, why don't you go say hello to the senator?" my mother says.

A vein on my forehead pulsates, but I know better than to stall. "Always a pleasure, Mrs. Mandell. Excuse me, would you?"

"Of course," she says, and as I'm almost out of earshot, adds, "He's such a polite boy."

"Like his brother," my mother replies.

The mayor's house is nothing like mine, all dark and earthy and warm. A mounted deer head above the mantel showcases his love of hunting. The senator raises his glass in acknowledgement when he spots me. I straighten my posture and prepare to perform. Like my mother, my exterior must be pitch perfect, flawless.

"Caught the game last week. You're a strong QB," he says.

His voice draws out memories from my childhood. Davis is an old family friend, one of my father's trusted advisors. So many hours spent together on the patio, in our dining room, in the hot tub, bullshitting, strategizing, cracking crude jokes.

"Thank you, sir," I say, allowing pride to show through. Even Dad would've celebrated my athletic achievements. Maybe it's not going to advance my career, but I *like* football—the rush, the challenge. Winning. "I think we have a shot at the championship."

"Hm," he says thoughtfully, disappointed. I brace myself for the lecture. "Really eats into your time, though. I'd hoped you'd apply that commitment to the debate team instead." The fireplace pops and hisses. Our shadows flicker on the wood-paneled wall. "You know, your brother was a natural. Just like your pops. I remember this one debate . . ."

I tune out the rest of his story. I've heard them all a dozen times or more, each a constant reminder of how closely Arthur followed in my father's footsteps.

Twenty minutes later, Mayor Mandell rescues me from the barrage of Davis's stories. He clinks a spoon against his glass and demands attention. "Before the senator begins his speech, I'd like to say a few words. Jim and I have been friends for two decades, and I can't imagine a more fitting man to run this country."

There is a grunt of agreement, a clinking of glasses.

My mother slides up next to me, the scent of alcohol

emanating from her skin. She leans in close. "Pay attention, Henry," she says, and though I know she's aiming for encouragement, it comes off more like a warning. The mayor's words momentarily fade into the background and all I hear is her voice, cool and calculated. "It's time to lock down the people who will further your career."

She's talking about those with strong ties to the community and the ability to make things happen for me. For us.

But all I really want is to get the hell out.

CHAPTER SIX

Anne

I fumble with the combination, tug on my lock.

Third time is *not* the charm. Almost a week in and I still can't get it right. I spin the dial again, pause as the numbers click into place: forty-four, thirty-five . . .

Shit.

"It usually takes me a full year to memorize my combo," says a voice from my left. A girl leans against the wall of lockers, small and fragile, like a simple bump could snap her in half. Her long strawberry hair falls over her shoulders in two loose braids. I can't remember her name, but I've seen her before. She tilts her head and it hits me. She's on Student Council, the token female—Samantha. Sam.

"Exactly why I never bothered with a lock at my old school," I say.

She grins, sarcastic, maybe a little shy. "Because you trusted everyone so much?"

"Never had anything worth stealing."

I spin the dial on the lock again, click through the sequence of numbers, focus hard on remembering the last piece of the combination: twenty-four. Of course. When the latch pops open, I yank on the handle. My locker swings wide, exposing bare walls, empty shelves.

She lifts an eyebrow. "I'm Sam."

Her smile is warm and welcoming, the total opposite of most of my interactions with the girls in this school so far.

"Anne," I say, and grimace at her knowing nod. "Obviously."

I sidestep an oncoming group of students waving purple and red pennants. One of them fake lunges at me, her Medina Greyhounds tee stretched tight across her oversize chest, and shouts, "GO HOUNDS!"

Sam shakes her fists in cheer, then turns to me and shrugs. "Football. Sometimes you gotta go with the flow."

"I'd rather go with a no."

"Aw. You should come to the game today."

I cough on a laugh, envisioning myself squeezed into bleacher seats as a bunch of jocks chase one another across a field. "Yeah, not really my scene."

Sam purses her lips like she's thinking, and I wonder what she's heard about me. One week in and I'm already rocking the boat, making waves and enemies. I wipe my sweaty palm on my skirt and pull out my tablet, pretend to study the interactive map of the school.

Despite Henry's personal tour, Medina Academy is a labyrinth of identical stone-covered walls and baffling intersections. So far I've managed to navigate by using the hanging portraits as guide markers. My locker sits across from the framed image of a past principal, the first female if I've interpreted the inscription correctly. Nancy Kratky.

"This place is massive," I say as a second wave of fans marches by with whistles and blow horns, forcing me to shout. "You need GPS to find the exit." I jerk my thumb toward the portrait of Kratky. "Currently, she's the only way I know how to find my locker."

"I've got Arthur Tudor right above mine." Sam blushes. "It's not so bad."

"I'm almost shocked his picture isn't above everyone's. It's like he was some kind of god." I look away, nervous I've offended or upset her with my insensitivity.

"He left his mark," she says simply.

I close my locker, secure the lock, stuff my history text and notebook into my bag, and sling it over my shoulder. "I've never had so much homework," I say, groaning. "And history is the worst. I doubt Ms. McLaughlin is the type to buy the dog-ate-it excuse, huh?"

"She'll cut you some slack if you go to the game."

"Nice try."

We start walking toward the giant school front entrance, my boots thudding in time with Sam's high-heeled click.

Above, the expansive vaulted ceiling crisscrosses with hand-hewn beams that might have come straight from a medieval castle. A line of evenly spaced arched windows offers glimpses of the lake.

Sam chuckles. "Seriously. Ms. McLaughlin is like Wikipedia— she knows everything about *every* sport. Want on her good side? Ask her who she thinks will win the World Series." She nudges her head toward the front office, where students gather around the fountains and wrought-iron benches. Sunlight streams in through massive windows to create the illusion of warmth. "Aaand, going to the games makes the office staff happy. Administration would mandate attendance if they could get away with it."

I chew on the inside of my cheek and glance at the giant Roman numeral clock on the far wall. How long could a game last? An hour? Two? "I don't know the first thing about football."

Sam's eyes light up. "Me either, but if we go together, how bad can it be?"

If the size of the tiny bleachers are any indication, pretty bad.

A half hour later, I'm stuffed between Sam and an obnoxious, oversize guy who has now dumped almost an entire carton of buttery popcorn on my combat boots.

Enormous foam fingers and screaming fans smother me. I don't get it—there's no one even on the field yet. I'm so out of place. The shimmery skull on the front of my hoodie sticks out like a homing beacon among the dozens of Greyhounds jerseys in the crowd.

I slink down on my bench and tuck my hands under my butt, waiting for something, anything, to happen.

Music pumps over the loudspeakers as a line of blond, anorexic cheerleaders run onto the field and take formation. Amid the sea of other Barbies, I spot Catherine and breathe an exaggerated sigh. Squad leader. I almost forgot.

"So I heard you and Catherine aren't exactly besties," Sam says, nudging my shoulder.

Noise blasts at me from every corner. The *thump, thump, thump* of feet hitting the bleachers, the hoots and hollers, the catcalling and cheers. I use the distraction to think about a response. It's not like I've got anything against *Catherine*, exactly. It's just past experience dictates I don't blend in so well with those popular, perfect, too-good-to-be-true girls.

"She's actually really nice," Sam says when I don't respond. "Unless you get on her bad side or hurt one of her friends."

I don't have proof, but I suspect Catherine's behind the rumors about me—apparently I've already got a rap sheet a mile long. My phone number is spray painted on every bathroom stall between Seattle and Medina—how original—and my affection for motorcycles somehow translates into a heroin addiction. In one creative spin on the truth, I sacrifice kittens and hold séances. Shit, if I was a boy, I'd be considered mysterious.

I'm certain the rumors are worse because Henry doesn't treat me like I have the plague, not to mention me publicly humiliating John. Their group is close—so close I'm shocked they're not stitched together. Piss one off and the rest follow? That's usually how it works.

The cheerleaders jog off the field to make way for the players. Maybe I don't get football, but my pulse sure as hell spikes when I see Henry in uniform. He looks up into the bleachers and I'm positive he sees me, *feels* me, too.

I try to look away. It's like my eyes are imprisoned, glued to his well-cut, impressive build, the way his pants cling to his hips and thighs. How his jersey accents the muscles on his arms. Funny that I never noticed his biceps before. I shake the fantasy of those strong arms wrapped around my waist and blow out a long, calming breath.

"That's the other mistake you don't want to make," Sam says, her tone a mixture of amusement and warning. "Catherine can be a bit possessive about her boyfriend."

"I'm not after Henry," I say, a little too quickly.

She shoots me a look of disbelief and stuffs a handful of popcorn into her mouth. Her voice muffled, she says, "Everyone is after Henry."

On the field, Henry bends over, waiting . . . for something to happen. Of course I'm staring at his ass. The play starts. Henry catches the ball with strong, capable hands. Extends his torso, arches his back, and throws downfield. The ball soars in slow motion. Ten, fifteen, twenty yards, I'm sure. The crowd erupts.

Sam stands to watch the catch and slumps when the one of the players is tackled near the goal line. "I'm not kidding, though." She turns to me, serious. "Catherine is the most popular girl in school. She rules this place—but not in a power trip kind of way. These guys have all known one another since elementary."

I cringe as Henry is tackled, wait until he stands and shakes it off. "I can hold my own."

"This isn't Hogwarts. The good don't always triumph."

Sam's warnings are starting to tweak my nerves. Compared to the raucous, obnoxious vibe of my old school, Medina Academy is about as subdued as a morgue. I survived. "Who says I'm one of the good?" I say with a mischievous grin.

I study the football field. Henry gathers his team in for a huddle. My eyes are trained on his torso, his muscular legs.

"Touché," Sam says. "So, new girl. You got any siblings?"

A response catches in my throat. "Just me," I say and swallow the lie. I look away fast, pretend I'm fascinated with something on the field, unprepared for this line of questioning.

"You're from Seattle?" she asks, pressing.

"North." My old house sat a few streets off Aurora Avenue amid a cluster of cheap motels and pawnshops. It was a weathered dump with low ceilings, short doorframes, and a leaking toilet the landlord used as an excuse to ogle my mother.

Sam blows out a breath. "This must be quite the change then."

She says it like I shouldn't be embarrassed by the past, as though it's normal to feel out of place, unwelcome . . . unliked here. My guard drops a little. "For sure. Any tips on getting through the culture shock?"

Below, Henry tucks the football under his arm and pushes his way through a crowd of oncoming tacklers. He dodges left, right, pile drives his way toward the end zone. Bodies fall all around him.

"Honestly?" Sam says, and we both stand to cheer Henry over the goal. "Stay clear of Catherine, her friends, and *especially* Henry. It's the only way you'll survive the year."

Henry spikes the ball to the ground. Touchdown! Fireworks explode from the sidelines. The crowd chants Henry's name and it reverberates in my head, tunnels down somewhere deep in my gut. He whips off his helmet and looks up into the crowd to wave. My chest balloons with ridiculous pride.

He glances toward me and this time there's no mistake. He sees me, too.

CHAPTER SEVEN
Henry

Arthur and I used to eat at the Medina Diner once a week. It's an old-style mom and pop burger joint where the locals hang out. While I ordered us strawberry shakes and double cheeseburgers, Arthur worked the crowd, increasing his supporters, his popularity, and his personal female fan club. Just like Dad. A slick smile, an innocent touch on the shoulder—bam! Instant follower.

Today, my mother sits across from me, out of place at the usual table, her pantsuit and pearl earrings an odd contrast against the torn checkered tablecloth. The scent of burned grease is so thick I'm halfway to cardiac arrest. I grab my shake and suck back a long swig.

"That's hardly attractive, Henry," my mother says with a cluck of her tongue. She lifts her coffee cup and swirls what's left, takes a small sip. Her mouth curls with distaste.

I don't bother hiding my grin.

A couple of guys from school duck in through the doors, spot us sitting in the corner, and fake a football toss my way. I mimic the catch and the room erupts with cheers. Residual excitement from last night's win.

My mother sighs. "Tell me again why you chose football over something more . . . civil?"

Because I love it.

"Try a shake," I say instead, dodging a repeat of a familiar debate. Anything to loosen her up. It's not just that she's overdressed. Her whole aura is too stuffy for the laid-back feel of this joint.

My mother runs her tongue along her top teeth. "I don't even know how you convinced me to eat here." She lowers her voice to a confidential mutter. "The atmosphere is absolutely . . . bohemian."

"Harsh, Mom," I say, wiping ice cream from the corner of my mouth with the back of my hand. Sure, the pleather upholstery is sealed in places with duct tape and the booths have seen better days. The neon signs advertising beer and soda buzz, pulse, and threaten to sizzle out. But classic rock thumps from a vintage jukebox. It's comfortable. Real. Something normal I can cling to. "Arthur always said the place had charm," I say, leaning on my brother's memory to keep her seated, at least until our food arrives. "And the burgers are out of this—"

The word hangs on the tip of my tongue as the restaurant door swings open. Anne and her mother stand at the threshold, eyes narrowed, scanning for a table. Anne cocks her head and pouts. I can't help it. Before I think about the consequences, I stand and wave my hands back and forth like an idiot until Anne sees me.

Our eyes lock.

She hesitates.

Maybe I should be nervous, wary of my mother's inevitable reaction, but it's like I'm someone else, someone decidedly not Henry Tudor. I motion Anne over and make room on the bench beside me.

"Mrs. Boleyn," I say, and point to the seat next to my mother.

"It's Harris now," she says, holding out her hand like we all need a reminder of her new status. Her diamond is blinding under the harsh overhead lights. My mother's skin pales, and for a second I revel in her discomfort. Mrs. Harris may be married to the architect, but she's not an equal—not by a long shot.

Anne slides onto the seat next to me and our thighs touch, a split second of shared heat.

My mother plasters on one of her "for the people" smiles. "Lovely to see you both," she says, though I notice she doesn't look at Anne, not even from her well-practiced periphery. "Your husband is . . . ?"

"Away," Mrs. Harris says, and sighs. "I thought it might be

a nice time to explore the neighborhood. Grab a quick bite to eat." She twists around to scope out the room. "This place is . . . charming."

"Indeed," my mother says, giving me an evil side-eye. I'm so going to pay for this.

Sweat dots Mrs. Harris's chest and forehead. There's a strand of thread unraveling at the collar of her faded black sweater. Though not as polished, pulled together, *regal* as my mother, there's something striking about her. Not hard to see where Anne gets it from.

"What's good here?" Anne says.

I hold up my cup. "Best strawberry shakes in the state."

"How about the chocolate?"

I shrug, try to suck more out of the straw, and come up empty. "Never tried it."

Anne wrinkles her nose. "Pretty cozy there in your comfort zone, huh?"

The slight twinges a bit. She hasn't known me long enough to make those kinds of comments, even if she's half right. "If it ain't broke . . ."

My mother fishes around in her designer purse and pulls out an embellished gold wallet. She digs out a hundred-dollar bill and hands it to me with a counterfeit smile. "Henry, go pick out a couple of burgers for Mrs. Harris and her daughter. I'm sure you'll know what's best."

"Oh," Anne's mother says, and presses her palm against

her chest. "That's generous of you, but I can get this. My husband left me his—"

"Double cheese, Mom?" Anne says, a deliberate interruption. I almost wince with her embarrassment.

Anne slips out of the seat, not bothering to wait as she
makes her way to the front counter. She surveys the menu,
the extensive list of burger combinations, everything from
plain cheese to Arthur's favorite, the Mexican. I come up
behind Anne, breathe in her earthy scent.

"Well, this is awkward," she says, not looking back.

I glance over at the table where our mothers appear
engrossed in conversation, though I can't imagine what they
have to talk about. "They'll figure it out," I say.

Anne orders two identical double burgers, loaded, minus
the onions, extra on the ketchup and Jack cheese, pickles on
the side. She passes on the shakes, asks for sodas instead.

"You're seriously not even going to try one?"

Anne presses her lips together. "Lactose intolerant."

"Oh shit, really?"

"No."

Fuck me. Played again.

Before I can come up with something witty, Anne pays
for the order, waves away my mother's cash, and sidesteps
down the counter to fill two paper cups, one with Diet Coke,
the other with a swampy mix of fruit juice and Seven-Up.

"Sometimes I don't know what to think of you," I say.

She raises an eyebrow. "Maybe you shouldn't be thinking of me at all."

Back at the table, our conversation is stilted, punctuated by long pauses. With each question, Anne responds with reservation, her tone clipped and terse. My mother's jaw is set, eyes flat—I can sense her annoyance.

"The mayor shared the final plans for the theater with me," I say, addressing Anne's mother. "The way your husband plays with light and scale is impressive. Twenty-foot ceilings, exposed beams. Brilliant."

"Thank you, Henry," she says, and her whole face lights up. "I didn't know a thing about architecture until I met Thomas. Now I can almost carry on a conversation without looking the terminology up in a dictionary."

My mother all but rolls her eyes. Anne's posture stiffens and I clear my throat before she can call my mother out on her rudeness. The girl's like a ticking bomb with a missing kill switch.

"Are you anxious about Harvard?" Mrs. Harris says. "Still a few months until early decisions."

"I've got to get in," I say, nodding. "I don't have a Plan B."

"Of course you'll get in," my mother replies. "Harvard is the best."

The conversation pauses as a waiter delivers our food, placing each hot plate on the table. The toasted sesame seed buns look like they've been brushed with canola oil.

Cheese drips over a thick meat patty all dressed with lettuce, onions, tomatoes, and ketchup. My mouth waters but I'm hesitant to dig in. I miss Arthur, and our regular ritual of who can eat the fastest.

"Goodness, this is a giant burger," Anne's mother says.

Mom follows with a disgusted mutter. "It's obscene, actually." She looks up at me and shakes her head. "Really, Henry. You can't expect me to eat all of this?"

"Not at all," I say, with a grin designed to diffuse her mounting frustration. "I'm just guaranteeing myself leftovers."

Anne shifts, takes a bite of her burger. Chews. Swallows. I'm captivated by her mouth, the tiny dot of mayonnaise on the corner of her lip.

Without realizing it, I've tilted my body so I can watch her, can observe every nuance of her expression, and I'm aware that while I stare at Anne, our collective mothers stare at me.

"What about you, Anne?" my mother says, cutting through the tension, deflecting my dangerous thoughts with razor-sharp precision. "Any thought to what college you'll be attending in a couple of years?"

Anne shrugs, her mouth full of food. She takes a sip of her swamp mix, swooshes it around a little. I'm mesmerized by her confidence and envious of her fearlessness, the ability to be herself.

"Anne is still finding her way," Mrs. Harris says, resigned.

"Our family has had a few set-backs . . . but things are start-ing to stabilize again." She smiles a little, and I feel a wash of relief when some of the sadness in her eyes fades. "It's time for all of us to move forward. Hopefully, Medina will inspire her."

"Wow. Could we not talk about me like I'm not in the room?" Anne pushes her plate forward, folds her arms across her chest, and then looks down as if knowing the position gives her cleavage a little boost.

My mother leans back against the seat and straightens. She bumps her knee on the table as she crosses her legs, tilts her head, tries to look interested. "And how are you finding the Academy?"

Anne shrugs. "Fine, I guess. It's fucking huge."

Mrs. Harris gasps and looks sheepish. I try to think of when any of my friends have sworn in front of my parents. Zilch. Nada. There's no way they'd dare.

To my shock, my mother waves off the curse. Moves in for the kill instead. "How about friends? I'm sure everyone in the school has made you feel at home."

Anne coughs out a bitter laugh. "Yeah, I'm a real social butterfly," she says. "I might have to start passing on invita-tions soon."

It's hard not to compare Anne to Catherine, who would rather starve to death than dish out sarcasm to my mother, to anyone in our circle, really. But there's something incredibly hot about how much Anne doesn't give a shit.

"Well, I hope you wait until after Henry's little party this weekend," my mother says, wiping the smirk off my face.

Sweat slicks my palms.

I open my mouth to say something, to admit I hadn't intended to invite Anne. It's not just the rumors, I don't pay attention to most, but there's no question she's . . . different.

Anne shifts to face me. "You're having a party?"

"Just some friends," I say. "Watch movies, play a little pool. Maybe start a poker tournament." I muster up my best *you-can't-resist-me* grin. "You should come."

Anne's mother claps her hands together. "What a wonderful idea," she says. "It's brilliant that the two of you have already become such good friends. Thank you, Henry."

When I glance over at my mother, she looks pained, as though knowing she's made a mistake and can't go back, can't uninvite Anne, or pin this slipup on me.

"Besties, right, Henry?" Anne says, and loops her pinky finger through mine.

Anne's touch ignites me from the inside out. We're two teenagers with obvious sexual tension between us—this is normal, right? Everything will be just fine if I don't act on my feelings. Not that I have a choice. Because if I cross that line, I'll lose everything.

"Yeah, the best," I finally say, though it's barely a whisper, and I don't dare look my mother in the eye.

CHAPTER EIGHT
Anne

A dull ache starts at the base of my neck, spiderwebs across my forehead, and thumps against my temples.

Thumps to the echoing *clash-clang-cling* of the pinball machine, the angry roar of a car chase reverberating through surround-sound speakers, the *snap-swoosh-pop* of the eight ball sinking deep in the pocket. Henry and I are tucked in the corner of his small poker room, but on the other side of the glass window, his basement buzzes like a sports bar, jam-packed with people I don't know and don't like.

I focus on my cards and tune out the background noise. Pretend it's just me and Henry.

It's not, of course. Judgmental eyes watch us from every corner.

Henry peeks at his cards, then presses them flat on the table so hard the tips of his fingers go translucent. This Texas

Hold'em tournament's been going for an hour and half already. It's just us now. Everyone else has been knocked out.

He checks his cards again, looks up. "You in?"

Trouble? Yes, I am. I've tried to avoid Henry and my growing attraction to him. Tonight, though, my willpower's dissolving like a sandcastle in the cold Seattle rain. I lean forward, not too far. Just enough so the strap on my tank top slips a little, showing off a hint of cleavage. He probably won't even notice.

I toss another chip into the middle of the table. It pings against the porcelain pretzel bowl. "Call."

Henry takes the top card from the deck, puts it face down, and then pulls the top three cards. He flips them face up with one smooth swoop of his wrist.

The king of hearts and two deuces.

Henry leans back and settles into the leather chair. His hair sweeps across his forehead, uncharacteristically shaggy and unkempt, and I want to run my fingers through it.

He looks up. Our eyes connect. I scan his face for a subtle tick, a glisten of sweat, a signal that his cards are good, bad, indifferent. Henry sports an epic poker face.

I clear my throat, tuck one foot under my butt, and lean into the middle of the table, stretching my arms, my torso, and dig for a pretzel. A subtle shift, a touch more skin. The AC kicks in, shooting cool air over my flesh. Henry's cologne mingles with the scent of popcorn and salt.

"You gonna raise?" Henry's lips twist, eyes glisten. Shit he's cute.

I cough out an awkward laugh. "Think you know what I've got going on?"

Henry's gaze lowers, hovers on my chest, pretends to study the royal bulldog on my Sex Pistols tank. His voice drops. "Oh, I know."

Hook.

I sit back, real slow, like an old film reel cranked by hand. Lick my lips. Stop frame. Bite into the pretzel. One crunch. Stop. Rewind. Play.

Line.

The pretzel slides down my throat. It happens all at once. Henry's eyes widen, a tiny noise squeaks out.

Sinker. His right finger twitches.

"Check," I say.

His head snaps upright and he gives me one of those double eyebrow raises. "You're trying to cheat."

"You're stalling," I say.

The minute hand jerks closer to midnight.

Henry taps the table twice, signaling a check. The next card up is the queen of spades.

My foot brushes against his under the table, lingering a second too long.

"Good card?" Henry says, all nonchalance. His poker

face slides back into place. "Got a couple of pocket aces or something?"

The winner takes home bragging rights, high stakes all around. But unless I'm imagining it, for me, for me and Henry, for us, the ante seems even higher. "I'm not that easy."

I weigh the odds against raising, calling, holding, folding. Bluffing. I was good at that once. But things are different with Henry.

Even though they shouldn't be, can't be, won't be as long as there's—

I sense Catherine before she enters the room. And then suddenly she fills the space, her shadow looming over us, everywhere that Henry is.

"You have to watch this guy, he likes to cheat," Catherine says.

She leans in and kisses Henry on the cheek. An innocent peck, sweet like candy, cream soda.

"Hey, babe," he says. I chew on the inside of my mouth. It's obvious he cares for her and I try to understand, to see what he sees. Maybe there's more to their relationship than people think, but I doubt it. I'm new to Medina and I already know this much: It's the sort of place where name and money mean everything.

Still, with her hair pulled back into a tight ponytail, por-celain skin brushed with effortless makeup, blue eyes, pink lips, rosy cheeks, I guess I get some of Catherine's allure.

Henry studies his cards, intertwines one hand with hers. Her ring glints, making me wonder if it's a promise of something, a token Henry gave her. Or Arthur.

"What's going on out there?" Henry says. He doesn't look at Catherine or take his eyes off the cards.

I really just want him to let go of her hand.

"I'm kicking butt at darts," she says. She holds one up for us to see, or maybe just for me, a warning. Oh, she's good.

I'm better.

I slide a few chips on the table, a decent bet, and ignore Catherine. "Raise."

Catherine yawns. "Well, don't have too much fun."

I will myself not to watch as they kiss good-bye. "I don't think your girlfriend likes me much," I say when she's gone.

Henry brushes me off, confused, or maybe just playing confused, and waves his hand in dismissal.

Four cards on the table: king of hearts, a pair of twos, and the queen of spades. It's looking good for me.

"Raise," he says, and pushes out a few more chips.

He taps his finger lightly on the cards. I listen for the pattern, some kind of Morse code. But I don't need the signal, I already know.

I raise his bet. Not much; I don't want to scare him.

My hand lingers in the middle of the table, hovering over the stack of chips. Our fingertips touch. Seconds pass. Neither of us moves, even though the voice in my head screams at me to pull back.

He calls the bet and turns the last card. It's the queen of diamonds.

Holy shit.

The minute hand moves closer to the XII.

Ten minutes to our curfews, ten minutes until this night, this moment has passed.

"You can do better," I say. He raises an eyebrow.

Maybe he didn't hear me. It's possible I never actually spoke aloud, never voiced what I've been thinking and feeling since the first time we met. Then his forehead crinkles, eyes go blank. Confused? Angry? Shit, I'm not even sure.

"I'm sorry," I say.

Henry sighs. "It's not that simple. You know that, right?"

I do know. He's trapped under the weight of expectation— school, family, *Catherine.*

I shift and our toes touch, innocent. A warmth unfurls beneath my shell. "Maybe it could be," I say, not knowing whether I'm talking about Henry, or me, or Henry and me. "Maybe everything's not as difficult as you think."

The clock tick-tocks, breaking the spell, and an old, familiar guard springs up around my heart when he doesn't respond. "Whatever," I say, feigning nonchalance, pretending I'm okay, *better* than okay. I'm fine, great, perfect.

I'm bluffing.

I push the rest of my chips into the middle of the table, wait for Henry to accept the challenge. He peeks at his cards one last time. It's a big risk, a chance to have it all—or lose everything.

Noise surrounds us. The *clash-clang-cling* of the pinball machine, the angry roar of a car chase—

Henry pushes the rest of his chips up against mine. Our eyes lock, a split-second spark. And I know.

He's all in.

I am too.

CHAPTER NINE
Henry

The oar slices through the water, propelling the rowboat with long, even strides.

I inhale.

Breathe out on the next stroke.

Recover.

On the seat in front of me, John mirrors my strokes. We shift forward in unison, bringing the oars out of the water, pushing back on the extraction. Repeat. We find our rhythm and surge against the smooth surface.

Morning fog hangs over Lake Washington, casting the tree line into silhouette.

The beach is uncharacteristically empty, but I don't envy anyone lazing around in bed. If it wasn't for rowing practice, I'd be pumping iron, running a marathon, doing something, anything, to ease the white noise of voices churning doubt in my mind.

Focus.

Seated behind me, Rick and Wyatt keep pace, their labored breaths punctuated by the synchronized splash as all oars pierce the surface in unison. Charles sits at the stern to call each stroke, eyes on our target, his bleached blond hair silvery in the muted light.

With just weeks before the fall regatta, we can't afford to mess up.

My heart packs an unsteady wallop—too fast, too uneven, too loud. A heavy roar in my eardrums. And buried deep, yet not fully out of reach, the seductive whisper of Anne's voice: *You can do better.*

As if on cue, Catherine's house emerges into view. It's not the largest mansion along the shore, but from an architectural standpoint, it's one of the most impressive. A single light shines on the lefthand side of the second floor. Catherine's.

The oar slips from my grip.

Too late I reach for it, hold on so tight my fingers dig into my palms. The boat jerks out of rhythm.

John curses.

"Christ, Henry, get in the game," he says, his tone sharp and annoyed. "That's the second slip since we left shore. Where's your fucking head at?"

The oar digs into the water and almost slips from my hand. "Let it go," I say.

"His donger's all twisted over the new girl," Charles says.

He laughs like he's lightened the mood, but tension spreads across my chest and pulls my intestines into a knot.

"Mind your own business, dickhead," I snap.

Charles is new too, less than a year in Medina, his family having transferred to the U.S. from Australia. He's got that surfer look about him—the perma tan, shaggy hair, laid-back, don't-give-a-shit—*shite?*—attitude. I haven't decided where he fits yet, but he certainly hasn't earned the right to just throw that out there.

He tosses me a bottle of water. I catch it one-handed, twist off the cap, and take a swig. Mercer Island looms in my side vision, an elongated patch of land lined with massive homes and trees so green they look like AstroTurf. We've got about a two-mile stretch to cover before we hit our morning target, then a full three miles back. School starts in just over an hour. Most days the time crunch wouldn't faze me.

"He's joking, right?" Rick says.

I don't bother turning around to answer.

"I mean, she's sexy," Wyatt says, and Rick chimes in with a low, "Oh yeah." Wyatt clears his throat. "But she's not the kind of girl you bring home to mom."

"Especially not *your* mom," Rick says with a dry chuckle.

"And she's definitely not First Lady material," Wyatt pipes in.

Because they're seated behind me, I can't tell if they're joking around, just giving me a hard time, if they're smirking, smiling, or on the verge of laughing. Doesn't matter. I'm not in the mood. I blot my damp hands on the knees of my sweats and grunt. Rising frustration gnaws on my insides.

"It's a serious question, bro," John says. "Something you want to share?"

I turn my head slowly to meet John's gaze. Eyes wide, jaw slack. It's obvious he's more worried than shocked. Why does he even care? He's not into dating—unless it involves a keg, a drunk girl, and the backseat of his car. Anne's not even his type.

"I'm with Catherine," I say with a finality that comes off forced and insincere.

The lines across John's forehead relax, and I can't help wondering if his relief has less to do with *my* reputation than his own desire. Shame washes over me as I recognize the signs of jealousy. No matter how much I try to dismiss it, tell myself I'm being ridiculous, I can't explain the dull ache pulsing in my chest, the sharp spike of adrenaline surging through my veins. I don't like the way John looks at Anne.

I grip the oar with both hands, resisting the urge to warn my best friend to back off and leave her alone.

Focus.

John picks up his oar, hovers it over the water. I catch him studying me.

My jaw tenses. "What?"

"You'd have to be blind not to see the way you two were

acting the other night," he says. "I'm all for checking out the menu, but you don't want to go from caviar to mac and cheese, if you catch my drift."

My blood flows hot. I let go of the oar, twist the cap off the water, take a drink. My teeth grind together. "It was just a poker game," I say, forcing the lie down with another long swig, working to control my temper. Truthfully, I've spent the past two days fantasizing about what Anne had on under that Sex Pistols tank top. I wipe the back of my mouth and toss the empty bottle to the front of the boat. "She's got a great poker face."

John scowls. "Yeah, she's got bluffing down to a science."

I don't respond, understanding him well enough to know he's still stinging from Anne's slight at the charity gala. He's not the most charming prince in our group, but this kind of reaction is over the top, even for his inflated ego—and it's wearing thin.

"Oh, come now, mates, she's a bit *bodgy* maybe, but she's no *dero*," Charles says. At our combined silence, he chuckles. "She's got a nice arse."

"That's debatable," John mutters.

"She deserves a fair go," Charles says, and looks away. "It's not easy fitting in around here."

I raise an eyebrow. "Yeah, I guess you'd know, right?"

"The key is persistence," Charles says, amused. "And an accent."

He's only part kidding. Family wealth and some mad rowing skills gave him a reluctant in with the guys, and white chicks pretty much throw their panties when they hear his voice. After a year in the U.S., the accent has faded, but every once in a while an unfamiliar word slips in, a reminder that he hasn't always been one of us, hasn't always fit in.

A little like Anne.

I shake my head. No, nothing like Anne. She doesn't come from money, isn't polished or refined, can't lean on an accent. She's hard, rebellious, and—

Hot.

Christ, she's hot.

My mind wanders back to that tank, the way the strap slid off her pale shoulder, further blurring the lines I'm already having a hard time seeing. I take a breath, pick up the oar, and stare straight ahead.

"Thanks for the concern, boys," I say with sarcasm, trying to regain control. "But it's not me who's spent the past five minutes talking about Anne Boleyn. Let's get back in the game."

As we take our first synchronized stroke and the boat lunges forward, I focus on steadying my breathing. On keeping a featherlight grip on the oar. On guiding the boat through the water. I focus on the silence, my surroundings, the burn of my muscles with each strong, deliberate stroke.

I focus on anything.

Except Anne.

CHAPTER TEN
Anne

Sam's fingers wrap around my biceps, tighten so hard
I'm sure the muscle will—

"Shit, Sam! That kinda hurts."

She drops her voice to a whisper. "Incoming."

I scan the hallway, squint into the Friday afternoon
crowds bulldozing their way to the front doors of the school.
"What the hell are you talking about?"

She opens her mouth, snaps it shut. A sheepish, ridiculous grin spreads across her face. I follow her gaze to—

Charles?

His tall, lanky body stands in front of us, blocking our
way. Locks of sun-bleached hair sweep over one ocean-blue
eye. When he smiles, his white teeth glow against the dark
brown of his deep tan.

"G'day, Anne," he says, Aussie accent slipping through his
practiced English.

Sam's posture straightens, her body tenses. Holy shit—
she's got a thing for Charles. He's so not her type, or at least
what I think of as her type, and the devil on my shoulder whispers for me to have a little fun. But Sam is my first, maybe
only, real friend in Medina and I don't want to piss her off.

In truth, I'm surprised to see Charles. Sure, he's one of
the nice ones, the only guy besides Henry who hasn't leered
or sneered in my direction—but he's still a friend of Henry's.
Of Catherine's.

"What did I do?" I say, smirking a little, positive the only
reason he wants to talk to me is to relay some kind of message, another warning to stay away from Henry.

"Nothing yet," Charles says. He winks at Sam, though it's
more of an afterthought. I imagine her pooling at my feet in
a puddle of desire. "But if you're feeling adventurous, there's
this thingy tomorrow . . ."

"No thanks."

Charles's smile broadens, a dimple appears in his cheek,
and for a second, I can't help but stare. Maybe I can see a
little of what Sam sees.

"Hang on, now. You don't even know what it is." He leans
in and lowers his voice. "Or who's going."

I fold my arms across my chest, waiting for elaboration.

"The party's at Catherine's."

"Definitely not," I say, my gut twisting at the mere mention of her name. It's one thing to accept an invitation from

Henry's mother, to hang out at *his* house—another entirely to willingly step into the lioness's den without explicit consent. Her sweet smile may fool most of the school, but I've had a close-up view of her inner bitch.

"It's a murder mystery," Charles says, like he hasn't heard me. "You know, the kind where everyone dresses up and tries to figure out who the killer is. Just come. If you don't like what you see, no worries. You can bugger off."

Okay, so now I'm a little intrigued. I'm always up for a good mystery.

Sam shifts, nudging my hip with hers, a reminder to stay away from Henry and Catherine and keep a low profile. It's harder than I thought. "Can Sam come?" I say. If she's with me, I can't get in trouble, right?

But Sam shakes her head. "Sorry, no can do." Her voice is small and shy. Sincere. If she was free, or could make up any excuse to *get* free, she'd jump at the chance to spend time with Charles.

Charles fishes his cell out of his pocket and opens a new contact page. Punches in my name. "Phone number and e-mail," he says. "That way Catherine can send you directions and your costume requirements."

Or the coordinates to hell.

"I think I'd better sit this one out," I say, reverting to gut instinct. I have a strong suspicion Catherine has no clue Charles has invited me to her party.

"You don't strike me as chicken," he says.

It's clear he's egging me on, and I'm too smart to fall for the trick. But then—

Something catches my eye and before I can look away, I'm staring at Henry. He stands across the hall chatting up some girl, his leather bomber jacket proudly flashing the Medina Greyhounds colors. He sees me.

My toes curl inside my boots with longing. My pulse races. Maybe I should worry about Catherine's reaction, consider the consequences of my actions, but as I tear my gaze from Henry's, I'm already saying "Yes." Sam's elbow jabs into my rib cage.

"Good on ya," Charles says. He enters my information into his smartphone. As he exits the contact screen, a picture emerges as the background, a group shot, maybe from the rowing team, Henry at the center, grinning, posing, making eyes at the camera. A lump forms in my throat. "See you there?" Charles says.

"Why do I get the sense I'm being set up?" I say.

"They'll give you a chance eventually," he says, all serious and sweet. "Take it from me, just keep working at it."

I bite my lower lip, dare to trust. Somehow I think Charles has some leverage on the whole fitting-in thing. "Why are you being so nice to me?"

He doesn't have to make an effort, doesn't have to care. Beneath those surfer-dude looks, I sense that he does.

Charles shrugs. "I know what it's like to be new," he says. "This isn't the easiest town to fit into."

As he saunters away, Sam blows out a breath like she's been holding it for as long as Charles has lived. I relate to the feeling and, despite my better judgment, try not to think about Henry.

"He's bloody amazing," she says.

"Careful," I say, and rest my hand on her shoulder. Look her straight in the eyes. "The janitors are going to need another bucket to mop your melted ass up off the floor."

She drops her head as though in shame. "We all have our weaknesses."

Which I guess is why I'm going to Catherine's murder mystery party, even if there's a strong chance I'll end up the victim.

"Catherine isn't going to like this," she says.

That's a serious understatement.

We walk through the exit and out into the bright sunlight. The scent of exhaust breathes into the air as the line of expensive cars rumbles up to leave the parking lot. A single yellow bus idles at the end of the lane.

"You want a ride?" Sam says. "Maybe I can convince you that going to that party is a terrible idea."

My cell phone chimes an incoming text. Catherine.

Shit, that was quick.

I click on the message and the attachment, read the

invitation and the directions to her guest mansion in the woods. A shiver of unease runs along my spine. There's nothing personal about the text, but as I scan my assigned role and the suggested costume accessories, it's clear Catherine has something malicious in mind.

Message received—loud and clear. Catherine's doing her best to scare me off, make me think twice about going. Well, screw her.

"Would you mind dropping me at the mall instead?" I say, and an anxious thrill runs the length of my body. "Looks like I need to do a bit of shopping."

CHAPTER ELEVEN
Henry

A magician and a blackjack dealer are crammed into the backseat of my car. Elvis leans toward the front dash and cranks the tunes, belting out one of his greatest hits so badly off-key it makes me cringe.

As for me, I'm trussed up like a turkey, stuffed into a crisp shirt and silk tuxedo, knotted off at the neck with one of Dad's old bowties. I catch Rick's reflection in the rearview and a twitch of envy crawls under my skin. More Criss Angel than David Blaine, Rick-the-magician embodies cool. Me? I'm predictable.

My shoulders tighten and I roll them forward, back, ease some of the tension. The fingers on my left hand drum against the steering wheel and my right hand grips the stick shift. The urge to jam the car into reverse pulses through my veins, swells with every curve of the dense, tree-lined drive.

Things haven't been right with Catherine and me for

a few days. Shit, maybe they never were. Tonight, no more dodging phone calls and making excuses—I'm ready to cut loose, have some fun. Screw everything for one evening.

I round the last corner and Catherine's "getaway" mansion emerges from the woods. It's an oppressive stone lodge perched on an acre of private forest on the other side of the lake. Light shines through the giant bay windows, creating the illusion of a wide-eyed jack-o'-lantern. Fitting. This place has always given me the creeps.

I park and pop open the driver's side door. "Let the fun and games begin," I say, emphasizing the sarcasm.

"Oh, hell yeah," John says, and his enthusiasm lightens my mood. His white pantsuit glows under the car light, the fake gold embellishments sparkling like stars. John's Fendi shades are the only real accessory on a shitty Elvis getup. Collar up, shirt unbuttoned halfway down his chest—maybe I got off easy.

The front door opens and a steady thump of bass winds its way through the tall hemlock trees. A bride emerges from the shadows, long white train in her left hand, wine glass in the other. I can't see her face, but her blond hair cascades over her left shoulder, and for one terrifying split second, I worry it's Catherine.

Rick slaps my back and I cough. "It's just Liz," he says, like he can read my mind.

I bite the inside of my lip to conceal the smile forming as we climb the stone staircase and cross into Sin City.

An enormous crystal chandelier hangs over a large blackjack table, and across the room, a bank of six rented slot machines clink, swoosh, and beep in competition with music pumping through a kick-ass sound system. There's even a faux stage at the back of the room. Catherine really knows how to work a theme.

A thin moonbeam cuts through the trees outside and filters into the room, out of sync with the whole Las Vegas feel. Only Catherine would turn her family's wilderness retreat into Glitter Gulch.

I'm about to ask Liz where she is when a flash of purple draws my attention. Catherine slithers across the room, the tight skirt of her fitted dress parting to reveal an inverted *V* of flesh halfway up her thigh. I can't help but enjoy the view. A silver band of diamonds crisscrosses her chest, pushing everything—I mean *everything*—up. My throat goes dry. Catherine is in her element here, radiating confidence and power. She's both beautiful and scary and, in this moment, I can't get enough.

She slides into my arms and nuzzles her head against my neck. Her lips are cool, wet. The honeysuckle scent of her perfume takes me back to our first date. And *poof*—just like that, I'm sucked in. "You look handsome, Henry," she says, a low growl in my left ear. She pulls back and sweeps her arm across the room. "Do you like it? I thought you'd enjoy the evening, given your recent *infatuation* with poker."

That's when it hits me—a humming vibration beneath my skin that lets me know something's not right. I scan the room and note the characters in this evening's charade. Elvis lifts his wine glass, the magician stuffs his face with caviar. The groom—*is that Wyatt?*—eyes a couple of showgirls, while his bride loiters by a theater-style red curtain chatting with Marie and Charles. The gang's all here. So why are my hackles up?

Catherine fills in the blanks. "We're just waiting for Anne." Her lips stretch into an exaggerated smile. "Things will really heat up then."

Frankly, I'm stunned—maybe even a little impressed—she's allowed Anne to come and hasn't crossed Charles off the guest list for inviting her. My thoughts are cut off by the distinct rumble of a motorcycle winding its way up the driveway. I move to the window, tilt my head. "That's her now."

I'm grateful Catherine can't see my expression. A dangerous twitch runs along my spine as Anne slides off her bike. My mouth drops open a little. I guess I figured the motorcycle was her unicorn. But seeing it—her on it—ratchets up my pulse.

Anne removes her helmet, whips her black hair loose, and slings a backpack over her shoulder. The short leather jacket rubs against the thin strip of bare skin where her T-shirt doesn't quite meet the waistband of her tight purple jeans.

Fuck me.

She jogs up the stairs, disappears behind a stone column, and then falls through the door like she's tripped over the top step. There's an awkward pause as she takes in the scene, and then her face twists in disgust. *Yeah, I know what you're thinking.* Her eyes find mine, and for a second, neither of us moves.

She snaps out of it first—it's always that way. "Sorry I'm late," she says, all apologetic and sweet. "Clarice was acting up." She raises her helmet in explanation.

Catherine jerks her head in Anne's direction as if she's a five-year-old. "Clarice?" The second "C" extends on a hiss.

"Yeah, my motorcycle. She's . . ." Anne's voice trails off. She shifts on her feet, loops her fingers through her backpack strap. "Forget it. Is there somewhere I can change?"

Catherine's face lights up like a damn disco ball. She pats Anne's arm—actually touches her!—and points her to the bathroom down the hall. "Take your time, hon. I'll just get things started out here. You'll catch on superfast."

Anne's eyes darken to charcoal. She casts one more wary glance around at the room before disappearing to go change. Tension binds my muscles. *Hon?*

"You're up to something, Catherine."

Her eyebrows narrow. "Oh, don't be a party pooper, Henry."

I barely notice as she gathers the cast of characters and reads through the instructions and rules, then passes out small yellow envelopes containing clues, objectives, and role descriptions. I'm a high roller—loads of cash, deep pockets, head over heels in love with . . .

I look up at Catherine and smirk. "You must be the up and coming starlet."

Catherine doesn't answer. Distracted, she looks over me, *through* me maybe, at something behind me, her eyes wide, disbelieving. Her mouth opens in a silent O—Catherine is rarely at a loss for words. A strange hush falls over the room.

Sweet Jesus. My knees knock together like they're going to buckle, and I break out into a cold sweat. A black and red corset is laced up tight against Anne's slender waist, accentuating the curve of her chest, her hips. . . . My eyes trace the path from her black lingerie to thigh-high fishnet stockings held up by lace garters.

Lust steals my breath, but it's anger that feeds my adrenaline. This is Catherine's doing, a pitiful attempt to embarrass Anne. I grind my teeth together and resist wrapping my jacket around Anne's naked shoulders and leading her away from the judgmental stares of our friends, from this . . . from Catherine.

Quickly, the lights dim, the curtain rises, and Elvis takes the mic on the stage. John swings his hips, really getting into character, but it's not *his* body I'm thinking about.

Anne works the room like there's nobody watching her, oblivious or immune to the harsh whispers and catty mutterings of the other girls. It's like she doesn't give a shit.

Meanwhile, I'm memorizing every curve, every inch of her bare flesh. And clearly, I'm not the only one. She slinks up to Wyatt, runs her hands through his spiked blond hair. At my side, my fists open and close. Though it shouldn't matter, the thought of her touching anyone makes me tense.

The power cuts out, plunging the room into abrupt darkness. It's pitch black. Still. So still the erratic beat of my pulse pounds in my ear.

A gunshot rings out.

Someone screams.

Anne's voice slices through the chaos. "Well now, sounds like someone's got a pistol in their pocket."

The lights flick on, blinding and fast. I blink, gather my bearings. The room spins, slows, comes to a full stop. And all I can see is red. Blood covers the stage, so vivid I taste copper on my tongue.

The King is dead.

No one moves.

And then, a twitch from the stage. John moans, sits upright, wipes blood off his face. He flashes us one of those crazy-ass grins, and relief eases the stiffness from my muscles.

Catherine laughs. "You're not a zombie, Elvis. Lie back down."

John's brow creases. "Aw, shit. Seriously? I have to play dead all night? Don't I get a drink or something?"

Catherine steps onto the stage, the heels of her stilettos

dragging through the fake blood. Her face beams with pride over the dramatic murder she's staged. She leans into the mic, wraps her painted nails around the base. "Welcome to this evening's murder mystery. Each of you has a motive, a reason to kill Elvis."

"Maybe it's his singing," calls Rick, eliciting a few chuckles.

Catherine carries on without missing a beat. She's a pro in the limelight, a glutton for attention. "Take a good look at one another, people. One of you is the murderer. You have until dawn to figure it out."

The music kicks in, and the characters begin to mill around the room. My gaze locks on Anne.

Yeah, I'm staring. So what? Who isn't? A slow smile spreads across Anne's face and it fills me with something dark and deadly.

Anne is off limits, but I can't stop staring. Can't keep my eyes off of her as she flutters about the room like a damn fallen angel. She sidles up to Rick, bends forward, and blows on the dice in his hands. It all happens in slow motion, one

long

extended

breath.

My jaw twitches. Rick's one of my closest friends and we put up with each other's shit—but if he doesn't stop ogling Anne like she's fresh meat, there won't be much of our friendship left by dawn.

Anne twists a strand of hair around her finger. Rick flashes her one of his infamous playboy grins. He's enjoying this, the role of bad-boy magician, the attention from Anne. Nausea coils in my stomach. The pressure mounts.

"Get a room," I snap.

Amused, Rick taps Anne on the ass. "Jealous, bro?"

Anne doesn't move, doesn't twitch. Why isn't she reacting? Does she actually like the attention? Maybe I've pegged her all wrong.

The air is thick with anticipation, as though everyone is waiting for me to respond, to deny the accusation. I can't. I *am* jealous. And that's bad. Real bad. Gawking at her is one thing—hell, in that outfit, who'd blame me? Thinking about her all the time, yeah, that's bad too. But acting on that here? In front of my girlfriend and our friends? I'm sure this is how a Stephen King story begins.

My gaze flits to Catherine and the noose around my neck cinches tighter. "Do you think we can continue the game now, or is there something else on your mind?" Contempt leaks into Catherine's voice.

She's egging me on, daring me to take the bait. But we've known each other since grade school and I'm better at this. "This is fun for you, isn't it? How long have you been planning this night?" I think about the poker tournament, the easy banter between Anne and me, the obvious chemistry. Maybe I should have hid it more. Catherine noticed. Everyone did.

And this is her way of putting Anne back in her place, proving she's not one of us. "I don't think it's me who's jealous," I say.

A chorus of gasps echoes through the static in my mind, but I ignore it. I gesture at Anne. "You can't stomach the thought of me spending time with anyone else, can you? You're punishing Anne because *I* like her. Isn't that why you had her dress up like a, like a . . ."

"I believe the word you're looking for is *prostitute*," Anne says. The blunt tone of her voice makes me take a step back.

"I didn't even invite her to the party, Henry. I only gave her the role," Catherine says, and there's an edge to her voice that creates serious fear. Liz and Marie slide into position, like two sentries poised for battle. Flanked by her best friends, Catherine is in control. Her eyes flash with challenge. "How was I to know she'd be such a natural whore?"

A muscle in my jaw ticks. Blood pounds at every pressure point. My fingers curl with thoughts of strangling Catherine.

But in the deafening silence, I know there's no turning back. I've crossed the line, put a serious chink in my Prince Charming armor.

Rick leans over to whisper in my ear. "Chill, man," he says, and squeezes my shoulder. "It's just a game. Remember who your friends are."

CHAPTER TWELVE

Anne

The defeated set of Henry's jaw betrays him. He's wavering, shedding his shiny knight armor and giving in to Catherine, to their friends.

I shouldn't be surprised, and yet the black hole in my chest widens. Maybe it was a mistake trying to beat Catherine at her game. I'm holding my own, but I'd have to be a robot not to be affected by her.

"You're so uptight, Henry," Catherine says, cutting the tension with practiced charm. Her face lights up and competes with the flashing slot machines across the room. Before I can even blink at her change in attitude, she's giggling, laughing so hard tears slide down her ceramic cheeks. "You totally fell for it."

The worry lines carved around Henry's eyes deepen. "What the hell is going on?"

Catherine steps off the stage and walks toward me, drapes

her arm around my bare shoulder. My throat constricts.

"It's a murder mystery, right?" Catherine says, projecting her voice. The crowd mumbles, guarded but supportive. "It's supposed to be fun. Not real." She turns to me, tilts her head to one side. Blond ringlets cascade down her shoulder, spill onto mine, like a thousand spider legs across my skin. "I didn't call *you* a whore," she says, and then turns to address the crowd, her people. "That was the jealous starlet talking. Get it?" She drops her voice as though auditioning for the lead spot in a B-grade thriller flick. "That was a demonstration of *motivation*."

The room stutters with cautious understanding.

"Bravo!" John sits upright, fake blood now turning his Elvis costume pink, and raises his beer in a toast. "Well done, Catherine. Well. Done." He shows off one of those cocky grins, shoots me a sick, perverted glance, and downs the rest of the bottle in one gulp. "Now, hurry up and solve this murder," he says. "My wig is giving me the itch."

"Better your head than your crotch," calls Rick.

At the chorus of "oohs," apprehension leaks from the room like a shriveling balloon. The music starts, the mingling begins, and the white noise of idle chatter fuses with the warbled ringtone of a slot machine in the corner. Henry's shoulders relax and his jaw unclenches. Relief settles onto his skin and flattens the stress lines across his forehead, under his eyes, around his mouth.

I can't believe he's buying her shit, letting Catherine off so easy. I scan faces, desperate for an ally, wishing Sam were here to see this unfold.

Gathering courage, I sidle up to Wyatt, lean in close, so close we're practically making out. The scent of sweat and whiskey leaks from his pores. The back of my throat burns with distaste.

"Why the sudden rush to marry Liz?" I ask, nudging my head toward the pretend blushing bride in the corner. Rick is working his fake magic on her, cranking up the charm, looking for the whodunit clues. By the looks of things, if Wyatt isn't careful, his new wife will disappear with the magician before the honeymoon even begins.

I force a seductive smile, trail my fingers along his cheek, keep up the charade even though I want to puke. "I hear her daddy's loaded."

Wyatt loosens his collar and sips his drink. The ice tinkles against the glass. "Sure, I guess you could call it an *impulsive* move. Not that it matters." He sneers, really getting into character now. "Elvis wasn't even a legit justice of the peace."

"Sounds like motivation to me."

My skin prickles at the deep voice that comes from behind me. Henry's breath tickles the backs of my earlobes. His hand brushes against my waist and I flinch as though burned.

Wyatt raises an eyebrow. "Is that an accusation, bro?"

Henry's chuckle sets my stomach aflutter. No matter how hard I've tried to stuff it down, I can't stop thinking about him. And dressed like this, I can't help but wonder what *he's* thinking about me. "Nah, I don't think you have the parts to commit murder," he says to Wyatt, and then points to Liz. "Now, your bride? She's a whole different story."

Wyatt spits out his drink and an alcohol-infused mist of slobber sprays my chest like blood splatter. I resist the urge to wipe it dry. "She does have some impressive balls."

"And what about you, Anne. What's your story?" Henry says, trapping me under one of those boyish smiles. His collar is loosened, crisp shirt unbuttoned partway down his smooth, broad chest.

A beat of uncertainty passes between us as I seriously consider the question and forget for an instant that this is a game, that I have a role to play, a mock mystery to solve.

His gaze rests on the slope of my neck.

"Just doing my job," I say, stopping myself before I launch into a dramatic monologue about my actual reality pre-Medina. How my real life drama is bigger than anything imagined in this room, so much more than my asshole father ditching me, my mom, his whole family, and leaving us alone and poor.

Henry's lips bend into a sexy smirk. "Were you sleeping with Elvis?"

I swallow the rush of bile flooding my esophagus as I picture John, disgusting, egotistical, slimy John, kissing me, putting his hands on me. But I have to tell the truth—because no matter how much I dislike him, I didn't murder him. I'm not the pretend killer in this evening's mystery.

I shimmy my hips and bite my lower lip, flutter my eyelashes, hating what I'm about to say. "The King and I did have . . . relations."

Henry visibly winces and my stomach flutters a little too fast. "Did you love him?" he says.

This time, I'm quick to tell the truth. "Fuck no. This isn't *Pretty Woman*. I'm a prostitute, not a bride-in-waiting. And anyway, what would I gain from killing him?"

Henry lets out his relief in a sharp breath, and we lapse into awkward silence. He snags a beer from a passing cocktail waitress. She shoots me a look I can't read. I think her name's Charlotte, but I've only seen her once at school—hanging on Catherine's every word.

"So, I know I'm not the murderer," Henry says. He taps his chest once for emphasis. "And I know you're not." He tips his beer toward me. "Maybe we should work together?"

"I could be lying," I say. My throat is parched. "So could you."

Henry raises his eyebrows—twice. Holy shit, he's hot. "I'm not lying," he says, and I search for meaning between the lines, a secret message only I can decode.

My face flushes. "Maybe we should compare . . . notes."

Henry nods, grabs a second beer. "Outside, though." He stares at me a little too long, eyes traveling the length of my half-naked body. My emotions ping-pong. "It's smoking in here."

I follow him across the room, ignoring the harsh whispers, the confused, shocked, and disbelieving stares. I weave through the costumes and party props, walk past Catherine, their friends, and follow Henry out through the patio doors, knowing now that I could, would follow him anywhere.

Cool air smacks me across the face. An expansive wooden deck curves around the side of the cottage, overlooking the thick forest. Beyond the trees, the night is many watts darker, darkest before the dawn. It should feel eerie out here in the silent night, but with Henry at my side I am somehow safe.

"You're cold," Henry says. He rests his beer on the railing and stands in front of me, rubs both of my arms with his hands. His touch will forever remain imprinted on my tingling skin.

My adrenaline kicks in when I look at his face, the way he tilts his head and watches me, an expression of wonder I can't explain.

"We can rule out Wyatt," I say, finding my voice. "And probably Rick, though I think he wants to headline at the casino."

Henry removes his hands, leaving behind a cool emptiness. He leans against the railing and takes another swig of beer. The bottle glistens. "Yeah, but since he's the magician, Rick could have just waved his wand and made the guy disappear," he says, a little tongue-in-cheek. "Guns are messy. Complicated."

He lingers on the last word.

"What about Kevin?" I say.

"Motive?"

Henry's face pales beneath the moon's soft glow. Music thumps from the speakers inside, but if I close my eyes, focus really hard, I can get lost in the tranquility. Can pretend it's just me—and Henry.

"Well, Kevin's the casino boss, right?" At Henry's nod, I continue. "So maybe he wanted out of his contract with Elvis. Maybe he wasn't making Kevin money anymore, so he wanted new talent. Fresh blood."

"Like the magician," Henry says. He grins as though I'm a modern-day Einstein. "Except we already ruled out Rick."

"If not the magician, then—"

A sharp rap on the patio window draws our attention. Catherine stands at the glass, motioning for us to come inside, her smile as fake as her sincerity.

"The starlet," Henry says.

The pieces of the puzzle click into place. We linger too long, savoring the refreshing scent of the outdoors. And suddenly, I want to explain, to make excuses for my costume—to make him believe this isn't really me. I open my mouth but nothing comes out. After repeated run-ins with John, even I'm beginning to question my motives.

Henry extends his arm. "Let's do it."

Catherine waits at the stage, her eyebrows knit in impatience and annoyance. "How nice of you to join us."

I slip my hand out from the crook of Henry's elbow, the safety blanket snatched from my trembling fingertips. Outside with Henry, I'd almost forgotten that I'm not welcome here, that I don't really fit in.

"We were mystery solving," Henry says with a wink.

Catherine's eyes smolder. "Do you propose a solution, then?"

Henry puts his arm over my shoulder. I stiffen, relax. Melt under his touch. "Yes, we do." He clears his throat. "Anne and I believe the murder was committed by—"

Catherine holds up a hand. Her lips barely curve. "This wasn't a partnership assignment," she says.

Henry feigns ignorance. "Wait, what?" He chuckles. "Aw, come on, Cath, it's not in the rules, is it?" He looks around for confirmation from the rest of the crowd. Rick grunts. Charles nods. The rest of the room straddles the fence, balancing loyalties. The back of my neck tingles with anticipation. "So as I was saying. Through our powers of deduction, we believe—" He pauses, hands me the floor.

My mouth tastes like cat litter. "That the rising starlet killed Elvis," I say.

John sits upright, fakes shock, and points to Catherine. "You bitch!"

The crowd hoots in laughter, but the atmosphere is ripe with tension. Catherine silences the room with one look, zeroes in on me and Henry. "What's my motivation?"

I swallow the responses that come to mind and focus on winning the game. "You wanted your fifteen minutes of fame," I say. "A headlining act at Kevin's casino. But Elvis had the gig—and his contract wasn't up. You couldn't settle for second place."

The room falls silent. Deadly still. I wait for the explosion.

Somehow, she pulls herself together—and I concede a point in her favor. "Congratulations, Henry and Anne," she says, her lips pressed tight. "I'm afraid we only have one prize, though."

"Give it to Anne," Henry says, oblivious to the steam rising from Catherine, the murderous expression on her face. She's not done yet, not even close. I fold my arms over my chest to disguise the slight tremble.

"Everyone, please, continue to indulge. We still have time before the sun comes up." Catherine's voice is light, but she's not fooling anyone. Especially not me.

She steps down from the stage, her back ramrod straight, her face a mask of perfection. She passes by me and lingers at Henry only long enough to issue a command. "Come."

Henry follows, glancing back with a shrug. Maybe he's not taking this seriously, but I recognize the signs. Never mess with a woman scorned—and Catherine is positively pissed.

My feet stick to the ground like Krazy Glue. A piece of me wants to go home, to leave now, before things get worse, before Catherine finishes off Henry and moves on to me. But I'm done being a coward.

Instead, I quietly follow Henry and Catherine to the bedroom at the end of the hall and pause outside the door.

They begin to talk over each other, their combined raised tones causing my head to throb. I should turn around and walk away, give them privacy, space to fight—

To make up.

"Why are you always defending her?"

Henry's voice raises an octave. "Why can't you just leave her alone?"

Catherine scoffs. "Why can't *you*?"

Henry releases a strangled cry. Something slams against the wall—a fist?—and I jump. I chew on my fingernail, debating, weighing the pros and cons of going in, staying out, walking away from the party, from all of this—

From Henry.

I step closer to the door.

"We can't go on like this, Catherine. Maybe it's time we accept what *this* really is."

Henry's gruff voice is muffled. I close my eyes and picture his eyebrows furrowed in frustration, the corners of his mouth tugged into a deep frown.

"Is it really so much to ask you to stay away from her? You're embarrassing our friends, and me." Catherine sighs. "You're embarrassing yourself, Henry. You don't honestly think she fits in, do you?"

I strain to hear Henry's reply. Wait for his white knight armor to clank back into place, for him to defend me, come after me, beg me to stay—

But their voices are now whispers, and the only response I hear is the *thump, thump* pounding of my heart.

CHAPTER THIRTEEN

Henry

Across the lake, the sun crests the mountain, reflecting yellow-gold stripes onto the rippling water. Medina boasts some of the most impressive sunrises in the state, but it's tough to enjoy the view this morning. While Catherine was passed out under the roulette table, I spent those hours lying awake contemplating and debating, digging for answers.

Catherine and I don't have fights, at least not the knock-down, drag-out screaming matches that land couples on reality shows. They just peter out. Like our argument about Anne at the party, which ended in quiet denial. . . .

Round two isn't going as well.

I kick at a rock wedged in the sand, waiting for Catherine's response. The color has drained from her face. She's like a teenage ghost—haunting and pissed. "I'm not sure I understand," she says, her tone clipped and controlled despite the visible tremble of her lower lip. "You're . . ." She pauses as though trying to comprehend. "You're actually breaking up with me? I can't even . . ."

"This is for the best," I say, casting her a sideways glance.

Doubt bubbles up like acid reflux. I intended to help clean the cabin and drive Catherine home, get some shut-eye before the Senator's gala I'm supposed to attend tonight—but I've made a necessary detour. One I can't put off any longer.

Sand squishes between my toes. Water splashes up and over my feet, all the way to where my dress pants are rolled at the ankles.

I stare at the waves. Maybe it was a mistake to stop here, the place Catherine and I shared our first awkward kiss. The memories rush back—her windblown hair coiling around her face, eyes bright with anticipation and remorse, the straight-up bizarre sensation of kissing my dead brother's girlfriend. Pushed together not even two months after Arthur died.

Something's always been missing between us. An intensity, maybe.

Catherine angles her body away, but not before I glimpse the wet streaks trailing her cheeks. I've seen her cry before. This is different, though—not manipulative and self-serving. It's frightened and desperate, like she knows this time her tears won't help, won't give her what she needs, won't give her . . . me.

I'm not Arthur; a shabby second at best. But I understand

the importance of reputation, the pressure of not being bad or failing our parents. It's one of the few things Catherine and I have in common.

"It's not you, it's—" I begin, and then stop. Because it kind of *is* her. She can't help who she is—who she isn't. I blink away the image of Anne in that corset, try to calm the unfamiliar flutter in my gut. I keep telling myself this isn't about her, that my growing attraction isn't clouding my perspective, but the lie doesn't sit right with me, as though pretending is somehow betraying Anne, betraying myself.

And I owe Catherine so much more.

I fumble for words, lean on clichés. *This is for the best. You'll be okay. This too will pass.*

Catherine inhales. "You're making a mistake," she says and reaches for my hand. I draw back before we can touch, before her familiar warmth changes my mind. But passion was never our thing. Shouldn't it be? I mean, isn't first love supposed to be more . . . I don't know, frantic? I think about what it might be like to kiss Anne, and a surge of electricity bolts straight up my back.

Catherine stares, her eyes bleak, and I brace for the inevitable. Confusion, disgust, and disbelief transform her skin into an emotional palette, a neon sign expressing just how deep these cuts go. No one is getting out of this unscathed.

"Henry."

She reaches for me again. I jam my hands in my pockets.

This stupid costume is chafing my skin, making me itch. All I want is to get out of this tux, but the look on Catherine's face tells me we're far from done here.

Another wave curls along the shoreline and splashes against the jagged rock bank to our left.

Catherine shoves her hands into the pockets of the gray hoodie she's wrapped around her dress. "I love you."

Maybe I'm a coward, but I can't bring myself to say it back, not in the way she needs.

Emotion gathers in the corners of her eyes. "We're good together. Can't you see that?"

My throat swells and I choke out denial. "No, you were meant to be with—"

She sears me with a warning look. My brother's name hangs on the tip of my tongue and leaves a funny taste on the roof of my mouth. She's wrong. We're not good together. We weren't even supposed to be together—that's the whole point. We were brought together in grief, an impossible, unsustainable connection, fused by an ancient, idiotic promise between our families.

We both know I can't be who she wants—needs—me to be now. I can't be Arthur.

"I was there for you," she says.

There's no denying it. Arthur's death blew a gaping hole in my chest, a giant cavern of loneliness Catherine struggled to fill for the past six months.

"We were there for each other," I say, gathering my wits. "It's what we both needed . . . then. But time marches on, Cath. *We* move on." Jesus. I never anticipated this being so damn hard. "What we have isn't love, not the forever kind. Don't you want to find that? Find someone who—"

Twists your insides into knots? Rocks your body with desire? Leaves you restless and hungry and desperate? I don't say the words, but it's too late. I've already tipped my hand.

"Oh. I see." Catherine snarls. "Your mother will never accept her." She twirls her hair around her finger to reveal the soft flesh of her neck.

Another day, another time, the distraction might have worked, might have lured me back into my comfort zone. But today, my resolve is stronger than Catherine. I have to do this.

"Anne is—"

I fill in the blanks, my temperature ratcheting up. Beneath me? Unworthy? No, Anne is none of those things.

"Manipulative," Catherine says, her eyes wide. "God, Henry, can't you see it? She's only after your money. You're a fool to think otherwise."

I remember Anne standing under the ballroom chandelier, surrounded by strangers, holding in her disgust and discomfort at having to put on a show, pretending to be enamored by insurmountable prestige and wealth.

No, Anne is definitely not interested in my family's

money. Maybe that's one of the reasons I'm drawn to her, knowing that she doesn't give two shits about my last name.

"She drives a motorcycle," Catherine says, as though this fact alone isn't fearless and sexy, but further reason to send her out with the trash.

Vulnerability oozes from Catherine's skin, tainting the air with bitter jealousy. I've seen this from her before, the kind of grief that transforms disbelief into remorse, anger into desperation, acceptance into revenge. She's a good person—she just isn't good for me.

A storm brews in the distance, a warning of what's to come. "I'm sorry," I say.

Catherine straightens her back, holds her neck high. "I thought you were better than this." She shakes her head and turns toward me with pleading eyes, one final act of desperation. "What happens when you get her? You don't want to do this, Henry. She will ruin you."

My jaw twitches. "You think I'm that weak?"

"Please." Catherine looks away. "Don't. Just give this a chance." Her small voice trembles, betraying her fear. A spasm rips through my chest. "Can't you see what you'll lose? *Everything*," Catherine says. "And for what? A fling?"

I know enough not to feed the fire. A cool breeze blows off the lake and ripples over my skin.

"It's cold," I say, and hold out my hand, hoping for her friendship at least. One last chance to end this without a war. "Let me take you home. You'll feel better after you rest."

Catherine breathes out a tired sigh. Her fingers intertwine with mine as we walk across the sand and get into my car. I can't shake the unease burrowing in my chest, the ominous feeling of emptiness that often comes with change. Being with Catherine is *expected*. What if she's right? What if I can't do this—can't be who my family wants—without her?

Catherine sits rigid against the car seat, her pale face clear of tears, wiped of all emotion. She leans her head against the cushioned headrest and stares vacantly out at the shifting landscape. I don't bother filling the awkward silence with assurances and promises. I can't take back the words, can't go back to a time before our first date, before Arthur died.

Before Anne.

As I pull up to Catherine's real house, she pushes open the passenger door and pauses. A long beat of emptiness hovers between us. She turns and rests her cool hand on my wrist. I grip the gearshift, trying not to flinch. She deserves the last word, even if I know it will be tainted with the raw pain of rejection.

"I'm not going to tell my parents yet." Determination flickers across her eyes. "In case you change your mind."

I open my mouth to tell her I won't, that it's really over. But she silences me with a hand to my cheek.

"You'll want to think really hard about that, Henry." She pauses, and I realize she's digging deep. "Because I know how much my father's internship means to you and your mother."

Catherine leaves without a backward glance. And only after I make sure she gets into the house safely do I jam the Audi into first gear. As I careen around the first corner, I shift again, increase my speed. The road blurs, merges into the landscape, and I want to scream. I step on the gas and hit third, letting go of the anger and the doubt. Slam it into fourth.

A wide grin creeps across my face.

I'm free.

And despite Catherine's parting warning, I am, in this moment, invincible.

My cell phone buzzes with an incoming text. I glance at the screen, prepared for the flood of questions and accusations, for one last desperate plea. There's no way Catherine will keep this to herself—even this early in the morning. But my pulse skips when I see Anne's name appear on my dash. A robotic voice reads aloud a text through my Bluetooth.

Hey. You ok?

A lengthy pause and the voice continues: *I feel like a jerk. It's my fault Catherine's mad at you.*

My heart hiccups. I resist the impulse to correct her, tell her this isn't her fault, that she isn't to blame. But we both know she kind of is.

Another beat of silence and then: *Anyway. If you need to talk later . . .*

I think of my mother, of football practice, of the Senator's gala I'm supposed to attend. I consider Catherine's threat and the lies she'll soon spread. I think about the responsibility that has been drilled into my mind, my whole being since my brother's death. . . .

And then, I stop thinking at all.

I pull over and text: *There's supposed to be a full moon tonight. Up for an adventure?*

CHAPTER FOURTEEN
Anne

My pulse hammers over Clarice's throaty rumble. Henry's arms wrap tight around my waist, hanging on like I'm his last hope, his only chance for survival. He's half laughing, half screaming as we hit the straightaway and I gun the bike. A little reckless in the dark, but it makes Henry hold tighter.

We cross the bridge and I ease off the gas. Storm clouds roll in and hover over us like guilt. Henry's supposed to be somewhere else, at some gala with his mother—but I didn't make him choose, didn't ask him to blow off the event to be with me.

"The bridge deck might be slick," I shout, with a quick glance back at him. Tufts of windswept hair curl out from under his helmet. His eyes are wide and shimmery, giant orbs of awe under the Plexiglas face mask. I love that he's not scared.

Clarice's headlights glint against the asphalt and skip along the white-capped waves like twinkling fireflies. Henry's body presses against mine, stirring to life those mutant pterodactyl wings in my stomach. We could go anywhere right now, ditch this place and go far, far away. But as we round the hairpin curve, I know that Henry would never really leave his friends, his mother . . . Catherine.

I try to ignore an unexpected cloud of sadness and focus on leaning into the curve, on navigating the potholes that could knock Clarice on her ass if I'm not careful.

"This is awesome," Henry yells. His excitement thrums through my skin and bleeds into my veins, firing up my adrenaline.

As we come up to the Medina Cemetery, I gear down and ease off the throttle, steering the bike along the narrow path toward tombstones flanked by a dark forest of hemlock trees. Under the shadow of moonlight, the branches extend like ominous arms, reaching out and drawing us in.

I pull the bike over and cut the engine. Henry doesn't move. He just sits there with his arms wrapped around my waist. His woodsy scent is so strong it catches in my throat, making it hard to swallow.

"Okay, not what I was expecting," he says, his voice a low drawl of confusion and amusement.

"You figured we'd go somewhere less haunted?"

I admit, it's an odd choice, but I want Henry out of

his comfort zone, the chance to give him an adventure, a reminder that life doesn't have to be boring.

"Afraid of ghosts?" I say.

His biceps twitch and push against my rib cage. "This place isn't haunted," he says, though the hesitation in his voice suggests he doesn't quite believe it. The cemetery is deserted, except for a mist that weaves through the maze of tombstones like souls waking from deep slumber.

Henry untangles his arms and slides off the bike. A chill hangs in the air, penetrating deep into my bones. Without the warmth of his body, I'm vulnerable to the elements, the oncoming storm.

"You can't believe everything you hear in this town," Henry says, and slips off his helmet. His hair stands up everywhere, giving him a Medusa-like appearance that makes me laugh. Under the dim moonlight, I see him blush and pat down his hair. It's cute that he's embarrassed.

I climb off the bike, remove my helmet, and bite my lower lip. "If you're scared—"

He shakes his head. "You calling me a wuss?" He pumps his eyebrows twice. "Or maybe you're challenging me to a game of chicken? That's cool. I'm in if you are."

"I like graveyards," I say, and for the most part it's true. I've read the brochures and heard the stories. This particular cemetery *is* rumored to be haunted, and I'm a sucker for things that go bump in the night.

"Me too," Henry says, and then adds, "from a distance."

Over the past couple of weeks, I've caught a glimpse of Henry's soul, and I can't help but wonder if beneath the entitlement and royal facade, the boyish charm and the sexy smile, there isn't something—

More.

I turn to face him, start walking away, beckoning for him to follow me deeper into the maze of tombstones and grave markers. My heavy footsteps crunch on wet orange-gold leaves that shimmer under the full moon. I tiptoe through the headstones and the crypts to the unconsecrated section, where early parishioners once buried those they considered "unclean."

"You're nuts if you think I'm coming after you," Henry says.

My veins pulse and I can't tell if it's because I'm afraid he won't—or terrified he will. "Plum crazy," I say in agreement.

I stumble on a rock, rebalance, and look up. He's taken his first step, inched across the soil threshold, and I know somehow that there's no turning back from this.

A cool breeze howls through the trees. The branches sway, giving life to shadowed limbs.

"Maybe we shouldn't," Henry whispers. "It's dark."

My breath becomes shallow. "You'll protect me though, right?"

His response is cut off by a sharp crack of lightning and a roll of thunder overhead. I barely feel the rain as it trickles down my temples and the back of my neck.

"Come on, Anne, we should head home. You don't want to be caught in a downpour. Medina weather is—"

I don't stop walking. The rain picks up and slaps me across the face, freezing in the drizzly October air. My bangs stick to my forehead and strands of hair cling to my cheeks. It doesn't matter. I don't want to go back, don't want to lose this time alone with *this* Henry, the Henry who isn't weighted down with expectations and responsibilities. I stand under a tree and motion for him to come closer. "We can hole up here," I say, and glance at the sky.

Henry ducks under the low-hanging branch and stands next to me. The current between us hums louder, drowns out the wind, the water, my thundering heartbeat.

Henry's lips are wet, his eyelashes glisten like dewdrops. Beneath his open brown leather jacket, a white T-shirt clings to his broad chest. My gaze drops to his jeans, the denim darker, almost black, from rain.

"We have to dry off a bit before we get back on the bike," I say, and try not to think about peeling off Henry's clothes, pressing our cool skin together for warmth. "We'd freeze."

"The old theater is across the cemetery," he says, nudging his chin forward and to the right. "It's boarded up, though. We'd have to—"

I open my mouth in mock horror. "You're not suggesting we do something illegal, are you?" Goose bumps rise on my arms in a way that has nothing to do with the wind.

Henry stuffs his hands in his jacket pockets, kicks at a rock. "Not exactly." He looks up and grins, an adorable sheepish expression that slices through the chill and creates an inferno in my blood. "My family kind of owns it."

Figures.

"The road is blocked. We'll have to cut across the graveyard," he says.

I think about making sound effects, mocking a horror movie soundtrack, some kind of *chee-chee-ha-ha* noise, but Henry's face pales. "You're really scared, aren't you?" I say.

"Nah." He pauses and chuckles. "Terrified, actually."

"I'll hold your hand," I say, grinning.

"If only I'd known it would be that easy."

"Come on then, chicken shit, let's do this," I say, and tug on his sleeve.

The downpour hammers us as we race through the cemetery, dodging tombstones, struggling for balance on the slippery, muddy slopes. Tall, wet grass wraps around my ankles and just as I'm about to fall, Henry catches me. We face each other in the smoky darkness. He studies me like I'm a science experiment, some form of rare species, and it turns my saliva to paste.

I lean my head back and close my eyes, savor the deep, pulsing ache in the middle of my chest. I can't remember the last time I've felt—

anything

like this.

I lift my head and our gazes connect. A magnetic current sizzles between us, drawing us together, pulling us close. My eyes flit to his lips, the soft curve of his mouth as it moves toward mine. Oh God, he's going to kiss me and I want it so bad, so much I can already taste the raindrops.

Lightning crackles overhead and Catherine's face flashes in my consciousness. I pull back. Clear my throat. "We should—"

"Get to the theater," Henry says, his low voice stuffed with emotion, confusion.

The rain has turned to sleet, and thin slivers of ice stab at my nose, forehead, the back of my neck. The rocks shimmer under my feet, and I focus on not slipping, on not leaning on Henry for support.

"There," he says, points to a clearing of trees. "Just ahead."

A tattered fence lines the horizon, peppered with an array of signs that read KEEP OUT. Beyond the obstruction is an old building—two, maybe three stories of brick trimmed with rusty wrought iron that bleeds onto windows boarded up with distressed wood.

"Around back," Henry says. "There's a window I can break into the easiest."

I shake off unease and nod, follow him around the building. A flash of lightning spotlights crude graffiti, chipped brickwork, and a low window crisscrossed with cut pieces of two-by-four. Henry bends and grips the wood, gives it a yank.

The first slat pops off the window. Henry struggles with the second, and then snorts with pride when it comes loose. He uses the end to smash through the glass and break away any straggling pieces.

"This would be backstage," Henry says. "The electricity was cut a year ago, but there's some candles and stuff in the storage closet." At my questioning stare, he shrugs. "We used to party here. I'll go in first, see if I can find them."

The thought of hanging around outside alone raises the hair on the back of my neck. "Screw that. I'm coming with you."

Henry chuckles. "Who's the chicken shit now?"

He slides through the window backward. It's a bit of a drop, but nothing that will break my bones. I turn around and stick my legs through the opening, call down for him to get out of the way.

Henry's hands wrap around my upper thighs and I freeze. "What are you doing?" I say.

"Helping," he says. His hands shift and rest right below my ass. My forehead breaks out in a sweat. I want to tell him to let go, that his touch is unnerving, distracting.

Delicious.

Instead, I ease down from the window and into his arms. I'm pressed up against him, his chest on my back, body heat melting through our cool, wet clothes. His mouth nuzzles up against my ear. "Stay close. I don't want you to hurt yourself on anything while we look for a light."

Stay close.

We stumble through the maze of abandoned props, furniture, the leftover remnants of someone's creativity.

A door creaks.

Henry shuffles around.

"Got it," he says, and a switch clicks. "I'm shocked the battery still works on this flashlight."

The room lights up.

It's a wonder we've made it this far without breaking a leg on a chair, or tripping over boxes and trunks. On the back wall, a line of mannequins pose in various stages of undress, their translucent, expressionless faces glowing under the bright light.

I turn away. "What are the chances we'll come across fresh clothes?"

Henry shoves aside a couple of boxes and drags an old trunk toward us. The brass lock is rusted, but open. He lifts the lid. "I'd say pretty good."

The chest is a treasure trove of costume pieces. Flared pants, intricate corsets and blouses, feathery boas, cowboy hats, gloves, boots. I pull out a top hat, and a long pearl necklace slithers onto the floor.

"How do I look?" I say, setting the hat on my wet, stringy hair.

Henry lifts the corset out of the trunk. "Smoking in this, I'd wager."

My throat burns as I think back to the murder mystery party and another image of Catherine flashes through my mind. I try to push back thoughts of her, but she won't disappear.

"You shouldn't say things like that," I say.

"Anne, there's something—"

I don't want to hear it. I can't stomach the thought of another reminder about Catherine, how they're destined to be together, how we can only be friends. He's not my type— too perfect, too rich, too popular. At least, that's what I keep telling myself. Because despite my better judgement, I'm falling for Henry, and that's a really bad idea. I dig out a pair of pants and thrust them at him. "You should get out of those wet jeans."

He hesitates, clearly unsure whether to push it. Resignation settles over his face and I wait for him to snap out of it, to get back to having fun and being carefree. He unbuttons his pants and I gasp.

Much as I want to see, I turn around and face the other direction.

"Suit yourself," he says.

I will myself not to look back and instead root through the trunk to find something I can change into, savoring each warm, dry item with the kind of reverence reserved for hot chocolate on a snowy day. I pull out a long, flowing dress. It's not my style, not anything I'd ever wear, but my options are limited.

With my back to Henry, I shimmy out of my shirt. My skin itches as though he's searing through it with his stare. "I can feel you watching me," I say, and slip the dress over my head.

His response is a strangled moan.

I shrug out of my damp jeans and kick them aside. As I spin around, I freeze. He's naked to his waist. A series of abdominal muscles form a path toward the sharp *V* where black pants hang low on Henry's hips.

"Aren't you cold?" I say, and then blink as fresh heat rushes to my cheeks, my neck. Holy shit, I'm dumb. I want to tell him that he's sexy and amazing, and that even though I know it's complicated—not logical at all—we should be together. I want to say it doesn't matter about Catherine, or his parents, or *anyone* right now. That it's just us—and that's okay. Better than okay.

Perfect.

But the words don't come out.

Henry's face grows serious. He steps forward and tucks a lock of hair behind my ear. Bends his face toward mine. I open my mouth to object, but my vocal cords betray me and we both go quiet.

I rise onto my tiptoes and curl my fingers into the hair

at the nape of Henry's neck. I pull his head down until his mouth almost touches mine. I don't think, don't breathe, but I can feel the deep rise and fall of his chest.

"Anne," he says, and his whisper tickles the edge of my mouth.

I clench my eyes shut and Catherine's face floods my vision.

Henry's tongue teases my lips apart.

Something inside me snaps. I can't help myself.

I burst out laughing.

CHAPTER FIFTEEN
Henry

A bucket of ice over my head couldn't have cooled me down faster.

"What the hell," I growl as Anne rips herself out of my embrace.

She pretends like nothing happened, tosses me a shirt, and starts rummaging through the trunk of clothes. She gathers items into her arms, focused on her mission, on not looking at me, even though I damn well know she wants to. Her mouth is pressed into a thin line. "I'm sorry. It's just . . . nothing. Let's drop it?"

Is she fucking serious?

I blink and she's gone, her silhouette disappearing through the door that leads into the main auditorium. What the hell just happened? There's no way I misread the signs, the tremble of her lips.

She totally wanted me to kiss her.

Frustrated, I slip the shirt over my head and tug on the sleeves, pull them over my wrists and try to shake loose the image of Anne's face so close to mine, our bodies pressed tight. It's enough to send me out into the cold rain.

Anne's voice echoes back at me. "Hurry, Henry. It's dark."

I chew on the inside of my cheek to stop from blurting out what I want to say. That it's her fault. That maybe she shouldn't have left me confused, embarrassed, and yeah, hot and bothered.

Screw it. I decide to have a little fun at her expense.

"Watch out for the rats," I call, weaving my way through the discarded props. My hip sweeps the edge of a table and a mannequin arm swings down in front of me. *Shit.* My heart beats like a loose shutter in a windstorm. "And the spiders," I say.

She doesn't answer, which makes me nervous. Like maybe she's fallen and hit her head.

Or worse.

I scoff, amused by my vivid imagination. My friends and I have been coming here for years to party, hang out, cop a feel. Still, I quicken my pace and round the corner. Freeze. An enormous shadow fills the doorframe, too large to be human. My throat constricts. "Anne?" Everything moves in slow motion. Blurry at first.

Unidentified limbs grow large and more menacing, hovering, threatening.

"Boo!"

My curse echoes through the theater like a damn lighthouse foghorn, and it's a full second as I gather my wits and realize it's Anne, not some ominous theater spirit rising from the empty auditorium. "Jesus Christ."

She punches my arm. "I couldn't resist."

The light makes her eyes go all shimmery and wet. Obviously I forgive her, suddenly lost, sucked in by an intensity that seems to live and breathe deep inside of me. "Anne, I need to tell—"

She's off and running. "Keep up!"

I'm wound up tighter than a mummy, itching to peel off a layer of guilt. It's like I can't fully let loose until I come clean about Catherine, my feelings.

I grunt and take chase. My head brushes against a fake hanging plant and dust spirals all around me. I sidestep boxes and mannequins and chairs, push aside the old creepy dollhouse used in one of the theater's last productions. Why does she have to make this so hard? I catch up just as Anne hits the stage and gasps.

"Oh my God. It's stunning," she says.

I'm trapped by the awe in her voice, understanding the sentiment. Even in its current state, there's a magic to this place.

The old curtain still hangs in huge velvet swags, the manual pulley system rusted but functional. I tug on the rope and the material parts to reveal two black plaster columns, chipped and faded with neglect. Anne's gaze follows the length of the pillars up to the ceiling where the gargoyles carved into the crown molding sneer back at us, their faces twisted into various expressions of warning.

"Interesting decor," Anne says.

I shrug. "The artistic director had a flare for the horrific."

Anne grabs the light from me and shines it on the graffiti-covered walls. "You performed here?"

I cringe when she hovers over a heart, Arthur's and Catherine's names spray-painted through the center in purple. The faint lines of a black X are scratched over my brother's name, still visible no matter how many times I've rubbed at it, tried to scrape it clean. I pause, waiting for Anne to ask about it, afraid I'll have to admit it was me.

"Once or twice."

Which isn't the whole story. Before my mother put the brakes on anything in my life that didn't serve her greater purpose, I spent hours on this stage. I've memorized every inch, the number of steps from front to back, side to side. The blistering lights, late nights, hours, days, weeks spent on props, costumes, and memorizing lines. The scent of dry ice and perfume, body sweat and adrenaline.

Now the place just smells like moldy wood and stale beer, and my entire life has become one continuous bullshit fairy tale.

Anne's eyes twinkle with familiar mischief. "I bet you played Romeo." She throws her head back, flattens her hand against her forehead and sighs. "Oh, Romeo, wherefore art thou, Romeo?"

She bites her lip and her eyes go cloudy. "Murder, tragedy? Star-crossed . . . lovers?" The last word trails out on an extended breath. "Romeo and Juliet isn't your typical romance, Henry." She drops her voice to a whisper. "Everyone dies."

She's right, but I'm rendered speechless under her electrifying stare. A soft smile lifts one side of her mouth.

I pull my gaze away and position the lamp so it lights up the whole stage. Plastic trees with black limbs extend and curl, casting eerie shadows on the floor and the walls, and point to the rusted metallic horse in the far corner.

"*Sleepy Hollow*," I offer in explanation.

Anne grins. "A forest, a horse. All that's missing is Ichabod Crane." She raises an eyebrow. "Unless that was . . . you?"

I shake my head and scoff. "I was never much of a leading man."

"That's shocking," she says, and begins to twirl across the stage. Her movements are jerky, like an uncoordinated ballerina, and I want to laugh, but with each spin, her dress curls up and around her thighs, exposing more skin. "There's a lot you don't know about me."

Anne spins toward me now, dizzy from the rapid

movement, and we crash into each other. She pushes back, her palms splayed against my chest.

And then she twirls away like we're dancing. I reach for her hand before she can go too far, pull her back in and wrap one arm tight around her waist, silently begging her to stay still. With my free hand I touch her hair. It's softer than it looks, even matted and frizzy from the wind and rain. I smooth her bangs away from her forehead and she closes her eyes.

My thumb brushes against her lower lip. "You're beautiful."

She rests her head against my chest, and for this brief moment, it's all I've ever wanted in life.

"I like you, Anne" I say, my voice foreign and hoarse. "A lot."

Her face softens. "Don't say that, Henry."

I tilt her chin so our eyes meet, so there's no question, no denying the words. "I *like* you."

"But—"

I pull her tight against me, understanding the root of her hesitation. "I broke up with Catherine. I can't keep pretending to love her, when I know I have feelings for . . . you."

Her face pales to an almost stark white and her lips part to form a soft O. Disappointment winds its way into my chest. I expect her to smile, to laugh, to give me some sign she's happy.

Instead, she pulls away, her expression unreadable.

I reach for her again but she spins out of reach. "Look, Henry, there're more costumes here," she says, and her voice is light, forced with nonchalance, maybe struggling for composure.

An awful tension squeezes tight in my chest. I hate that I can't read her, can't decipher her thoughts, her feelings about me.

She pulls an item of clothing out of a rusted costume trunk. "Oh, this is perfect."

"Anne?"

She looks up. Her eyes are manic, wide and dark, her pupils dilated into twin black pools. "I like you too, Henry. A lot. I just need a few seconds to . . . think."

Helpless, I nod.

"Go, sit," she says, pointing a finger toward the empty auditorium. Beer stains and stale popcorn kernels spot broken red-velvet seats. Armrests busted loose, seat backings ripped and torn—most of them barely chairs at all.

Anne ducks behind one of the pillars and peers around the corner, her face flushed. "It's my turn to perform on this stage."

I'm relieved at the return of her carefree self. "There's no music, no—"

The protest dies on my lips as Anne emerges wearing a sheer black skirt, the material so thin I can see the outline of her dark panties, the pink tinge of her bare thighs. A tight shirt stretches across her chest, stops midstomach to reveal a wide band of skin. A silver cross dangles from her belly button.

"Aren't you going to sit?" Anne says.

My mouth is bone dry. "I'd rather stare."

Still, I choose one of the side seats in the front row and settle in, rest my palms on my thighs. Bounce my knees. Holy shit, I can't sit still. I consider moving to a more comfortable chair but Anne glides to center stage, starts moving her hips.

She sways in slow motion, chewing on her fingernails like she's unsure. A little scared. It's such a stark contrast to her normal confidence, I don't recognize my cue. "Play something," she says, nervous and shy.

I fumble for my phone, flip to my playlist, pick the first song. It's loud and obnoxious and blasts into the theater with the force of a heavy metal band. *Shit.* I hit stop, scramble for something else, something smoother, slower, sexier, terrified she'll change her mind if I hesitate.

I hit play.

Anne begins to dance, hesitant at first, the steps awkward and cute. And then, it's as if she's swept up in the moment and the music, under some kind of spell. She closes her eyes and bends at the knees, slithers up to standing position. Dances forward and back, close and then far away.

A shudder vibrates up my spine, and along with the excitement comes the reckless thrill of adrenaline.

Raindrops smear the upper theater windows, grounding me in this moment, this fantasy. And as I watch, the swollen tightness in my chest begins to unravel, unwinding the fragile knot around my heart.

Anne descends the stairs, inching toward me until she stands at my feet, our knees touching. The theater shrinks, closes in around us. She bends toward me and I pull her so close that our foreheads touch. Terrified she'll run again, I barely breathe.

"You're sure?" she says, her voice catching a little.

"I've never been more sure of anything," I say, and it's true. Logic tells me to wait, give Catherine, our friends, my mother, time to adjust. But how do you slow down the inevitable?

She climbs onto the seat, her knees pushed against the cushion on either side of my legs. Heat burns through my pants and scorches my skin. Her mouth hovers over mine, an invitation.

I lean forward, my voice caught in my throat, and press my lips against hers. Hers are warm and soft, her breath sweet. I weave my fingers through her hair, grab the back of her neck, and pull her close. Her tongue sweeps across my lower lip, and the metallic ball of her piercing scrapes my flesh.

I'm shocked by how good it feels not to think. To get totally lost. In her.

It's strange when you're not happy for so long, and then suddenly you're—

Alive.

Anne puts her hands on my chest, moving her fingers so that my flesh tingles and sweats. I pull her close, tuck her head under my chin, forgetting in this moment the obstacles and complications ahead. "This won't be easy," I say.

"I know." Her hand works its way under my shirt, slides over my chest and stomach, down under the waistband of my pants. My skin is on fire. "Is this easy?"

I close my eyes and nod, surrender to her touch. "You're worth the trouble."

"Then, for now, let this be enough."

CHAPTER SIXTEEN

Anne

The porch light glows through the trees, an unfamiliar beacon drawing me . . . home. The sentiment doesn't sit right, kind of lodges in the back of my throat. It's too soon to stop smiling, to stop thinking of Henry, our date, the feeling of—

A blush creeps up my neck.

I pull Clarice over at the bottom of the driveway, cut the engine, and slide off my helmet. Listen. I half expect my mother's voice to slice through the eerie silence. I'm two hours past curfew on a school night, sopping wet and grinning like a damned fool.

Cold rain trickles down the back of my neck. I strap my helmet onto the seat and start pushing the bike up the driveway to keep the noise down. Pebbles, branches, and wet leaves *crack-crackle-snap* under my boots and Clarice's tires.

Lake Washington shimmers in the background. A handful

of lights twinkle through the pitch-dark shoreline, like distant fireflies too restless for sleep. I inhale air that smells clean and fresh, untainted by the greasy scent of the fast food joint at the end of my old street. On the other side of the lake, stars blink from behind retreating storm clouds.

I lean Clarice up against the garage. I'm not allowed to park her next to Thomas's expensive car or my mother's new BMW, as though Clarice's very presence will somehow cheapen the other vehicles.

Tonight, even this doesn't annoy me.

I sling my backpack over my shoulder and creep up the sidewalk. The whole house is dark, quiet, tucked in under the thick cover of night. I insert my key into the lock and open the door with a gentle push.

Blinking, I adjust my eyes to the lighting in the grainy hallway as I bend to untie my boots, edge them off my bare feet. Dried mud flakes onto the tile floor. Still beaming, I slide off my wet jacket and tiptoe to the bathroom for a towel to clean up the mess.

The sitting room lamp switches on and I gasp.

"Quite late for your curfew, aren't you, Anne?"

My back stiffens at the sound of my stepfather's disapproving voice. "Shit," I hiss, my hand moving to cover my chest. My pulse pounds in my ears.

Thomas sits in an enormous wingback chair, hands wrapped around the armrests, legs bent with rigid formality.

There's an empty bourbon glass on the side table and I wonder how much he's had to drink, whether I'm in for a fight or quiet admonishment. My gaze flits to the coffee table where the final plans for the new creative center are spread across the surface, a complex tangle of lines and sharp angles.

"Working late?" I say, and tuck a strand of wet hair behind my ear. My skin is cool, goose pimpled. I can hardly stand still thinking about curling into bed and calling Henry.

"Where have you been?"

The truth balances on the edge of my lips, but I bite down. I don't know how Thomas will react to my date with Henry, if he'll be happy, relieved, or angrier than hell. It doesn't matter. I'm not ready to share.

"Exploring." I consider telling him about the cemetery, the theater, and the intriguing Medina landmarks I've passed, but even that feels too sacred. "This town is bigger than it looks."

"Your mother was worried," he says. He leans forward as though to stand, but rests his forearms on his knees instead. Interlaces his fingers. His meaty thumbs rub absently against each other and he bows his head. "I don't like it when she's upset. She doesn't sleep. I had to give her a pill." He glances over at the grandfather clock in the corner. "She's been out for half an hour."

I should feel guilty, but the emotion lies dormant, stifled by a range of feelings I can't identify. The air in my lungs escapes in a shuddering, long breath. "I lost track of time."

Thomas pauses for what seems an eternity. "And you weren't concerned about riding your motorcycle in the storm?" He holds my gaze and my blood runs cold. Busted.

I consider the best phrasing, some kind of excuse. "I pulled over and found shelter, waited out the worst of it."

The tension between us hums, stretches out for seconds, minutes—

"It's very important to your mother that you fit in here," Thomas says. My spine straightens and my lips press together in a firm line. It's so much harder to "fit in here" than everyone thinks. I'm expecting a lecture, but Thomas softens his tone, like he wants us to be best buddies. Worried, maybe, that if he pushes too much, I'll snap. "I want that too. I want both of you to like it here. We're a family now."

He loves knowing he swooped in to rescue Mom from certain destitution, scooped us out of a Jerry Springer episode and planted us here in this cold, stone-walled castle. My mother's knight in shining armor. I don't even know if she truly loves him—or if his proposal simply gave her an out, a way to forget the dysfunctions of our fractured family. Yesterday I might have told Thomas to fuck off, that we never needed him to save us, aren't ready to move on, but tonight, I think about Henry, about the future, and maybe there's a twinge of gratitude. Because if it wasn't for Thomas and his white limousine, there'd be no Henry.

A deep pulsing ache fills my chest, a reckless need to

return to the theater, to the safety of Henry's arms.

"And I want that too," I say calmly, unwilling to let him hear the desperation in my admission. "I like the school. It's . . . huge. And my chem teacher is funny." I chew on the inside of my cheek, waiting to see if he needs more convincing. Thomas nods but I keep going, suddenly compelled to prove that I'm making an effort. "I have this new friend, Sam. She's on Student Council—the, uh, secretary. I think you and Mom would like her." I clear my throat. "And I've been invited to a few parties, even a murder mystery." My smile is authentic, encouraging.

Thomas stands. "Good. It sounds like you're on the right track, then. Your mother and I just want to make sure you stay there. No repeats of the past."

His meaning hovers in the air like a ghostly apparition. Anger burns its way up my esophagus. Which version of the story does he believe? Whose side is he really on? My body goes hot with the need to defend myself. I don't like the way he's lumped himself in with Team Mom.

Instead I just say, "Yes, sir."

Thomas grunts. "School tomorrow. You head on up to bed now."

I turn, but he stops me with a warm hand on my shoulder. His voice is low and gravelly, infused with an underlying hint of warning. "Let me deal with your mother. I'll assure her that this won't happen again."

Thomas shuts off the light, and when he finally retreats to the main floor master suite, I climb the long staircase to my bedroom on the second floor, his words, the warning, echoing in my mind: *I'll assure her that this won't happen again.*

A blast of cool air hits me as I cross the threshold of my new bedroom. Gauzy curtains hover at the open window, damp from the wind and rain. Despite the chill, I'm comforted knowing no one has been in here, pawing through my shit for clues to where I've been.

Not that they'd find much. I've thrown out or left behind most of my personal things—my old Goth art and glam rock posters would shock the simple palette of my new space. A walk-in closet overflows with clothes I won't wear and heels more suited for stabbing someone than walking in.

I peer out into the darkness. Henry's house hides somewhere in the distance, invisible through the thick forest of trees that separates us. Below, the soft glow of the yard lights shine over the labyrinth of perfectly trimmed hedges and the rose garden that surrounds the white latticework gazebo at the end of the grass. Grass so meticulous I'm afraid to walk across it.

I pull the window shut and slide the curtains into place, turn on the bedside lamp, and fold back the thick duvet. I strip down to my underwear and tanktop, crawl into bed, pulling the blankets up around my neck, cell phone gripped tight in my palm.

Finally, I send Henry a text.

CHAPTER SEVENTEEN
Henry

My mother breathes in like she's trying to make herself taller, more authoritative. Then her mouth goes small, a sign she's trying not to erupt and say something she might regret.

I'm used to feeling like I'll never measure up. I can't recall the last time she wasn't annoyed or sad or disappointed. But this level of anger . . .

She doesn't yell. Just closes her eyes and inhales deeply, like she's aiming for patience. There's something scary about my mother's silences that makes you wish she'd just scream and get it all out.

"Can you imagine," she says, her voice small and tight, jaw clenched. Every word comes out like an extended syllable. "My embarrassment? My utter shock?"

She lowers herself onto a chair and cups her hands around a glass of red wine. "I don't understand," she starts, and I know what's coming, brace for the fallout. "Catherine is perfect for you. I expected you to get married. Everyone did."

I slide out of my jacket, still damp from the rain, and fold it across my lap as I sit at one of the kitchen chairs, careful not to get the white cushion dirty. The spicy tang of Anne's perfume lingers on the fabric. "It may as well have been an arranged engagement," I say, softening my voice to take the sting out of my next sentence. "Catherine was perfect for Arthur, Mom. Not me."

My mother often wields her sadness like a weapon. But this time, I don't duck.

"Did you even give it a chance?" she says. "You're still in high school. You would have loved each other in time."

Love. I'm not even sure I understand what that word means, but it sure as hell isn't what I felt about Catherine. "How much time, Mom?" I lean across the table and take one of her hands in mine, tilt my head so our eyes lock and she can't escape the question. "We have nothing in common."

"She's a beautiful young girl with a bright future ahead of her," my mother says.

"Which is why I know she'll be just fine," I say.

"Her father will never give you an internship now."

I nod. "I know. There are other ways—"

She leans back and starts picking at something on her blouse. Her pantsuit is wrinkled, like she's been wearing it a few hours too long.

Cut through the tension and it's plain to see her anger isn't rooted in my failed relationship. Not really. Sure, she's pissed that I blew off the gala, that I apparently missed an important, surprise meeting with a Harvard VIP. But even that's not the core of her frustration.

The real problem is that I didn't tell her about Catherine—someone else did. And since I wasn't there, it provided undeniable proof that, despite pretending, my mother and I aren't as close anymore, that her influence isn't as substantial as some may have been led to believe.

Guilt winds its way down my throat and settles on my chest, making me feel heavy with responsibility and longing. Our relationship has changed so much, no more the simple bond between mother and son, but rather a complex business partnership, with her holding on with an iron fist.

"I should have called," I say.

She glances up at the giant clock over the china cabinet. The minute hand clicks past midnight. My phone vibrates in my pocket and I know it's Anne, texting to say she got home safe, waiting for me to call and whisper good night.

Mother swirls her wine, downs what's left. "So, where have you been?"

I hesitate a second too long. She pushes her glass aside with disgust and stands. Begins to pace the narrow length of the kitchen. "It's true then? The rumors . . . about her?"

"Mom . . ." I run my hand through the disheveled mess of

my hair and squeeze the back of my neck. Tension pulls my muscles into knots. "It's not what you think."

Except that it is, and she damn well knows it.

"I don't know what to think anymore, Henry." She throws her arms up, then presses the heel of one palm to her forehead. Closes her eyes. "It's like you've forgotten who you are. The person you're *meant* to be."

My voice rises an octave as frustration gives way to anger. "And who is that, exactly? Arthur? Because in case you haven't noticed, he's dead."

She whips her head around and silences me with a glare. "At least there's something we agree on. Arthur would never have disrespected the family, thrown all of our hard work in my face."

"I missed an event, Mom. It's not like I dropped out of school or murdered someone."

Normally when my mother brings up Arthur, all I feel is guilt. But right now I feel indignant, empowered even. My phone vibrates again, sending a tingle into my legs. If I don't call Anne soon, she'll worry something's wrong.

"I should have been the one to tell you about Catherine." I fold my jacket over my arm and stand. My knees buckle a little. "And maybe I shouldn't have gone out with Anne tonight." The words sound insincere on my tongue, a thinly veiled apology.

My mother tilts her head like she's stargazing. "I just don't understand what's gotten into you, Henry."

"I'll contact the Harvard guy," I say. "Set up a lunch or something." I attempt a smile. "You know I can woo him."

My mother carries her glass to the fridge, fills it with cool water. She takes a long drink and sets the glass on the counter with a soft clink. She doesn't look at me as she says, "I don't approve of that Boleyn girl. She isn't right for this family. Or you."

I'm tired of hearing that, from Catherine, from my best friends, from my mother. None of them know her. They can't *feel* what I do when I'm with her.

"If you'd just give her a chance, you'd see—"

What? Anne wears her rebellion like warrior paint. That's all my mother sees.

Resigned, I lean against the counter and wait. I always cave first, desperate for some way to ease the sadness. But there is nothing I can do to fill Arthur's void. And for tonight, I've given up trying.

"You're so close, Henry. Your career, Harvard, everything you want, is *right* there."

"No, Mom, everything *you* want is right there," I say. When she recoils, I slump my shoulders. Back off. "I love you."

Her eyes well, but the tears don't fall. I wonder if she's even capable of crying anymore. "You are my son," she says.

"And I trust you will do the right thing. I know you will make me—and your father, God rest his soul—proud."

I nod, wishing the *right* thing meant the same to all of us.

But as she turns off the kitchen light and leaves me alone in the dark, my cell phone vibrates again and I know that as long as I am with Anne, there's no hope of making my mother proud.

CHAPTER EIGHTEEN

Anne

I t's happening so fast. My feelings for Henry grow and swell, pushing against my heart. I've become one of those dopey girls, delirious and stupid with love.

Last night Henry and I texted for hours, almost until dawn. I'm wrung out, running on empty, and so happy. So ridiculously happy.

As I fumble to open my locker and shove my textbooks inside, a thick envelope floats to the floor. My name is scrawled on the front, the bold black lettering punctuated with a hand-drawn heart.

I slide my thumb under the seal and peer inside. The note is folded like origami, but even so, I can see through to the ink on the other side. My fingers tremble as I unfold and unfold and unfold until there is a full sheet of paper and . . . a locket? I pinch the thin chain between two fingers and hold it upright so it unravels to reveal a small heart held together by a tiny hinge. My fingers fumble to undo it, the pterodac-tyl wings in my stomach growing larger, bashing against my sternum until—

The heart splits in half.

H+A is written in blue ink on a slip of paper tucked inside.

My smile nearly stretches my cheeks out of shape as I clasp the locket back together, tuck it in my hand, and read Henry's note.

> *Anne,*
> *I've got rowing practice during lunch, but maybe this*
> *heart will keep me in yours. It was my grandmother's. I*
> *can't wait to see you again.*
> *—H*
> *PS: Don't be alarmed that I broke into your locker.*
> *Being Student Council president comes with a few*
> *perks.*

I fold the note into a tight square and stuff it in my front pocket. My lips are so dry from smiling, I'm convinced they'll crack, but no matter how hard I try to stop, the grin won't go away.

Distracted, I'm jostled from behind and pitched forward into my locker. My head hits the metal shelf. "What the—" I say, turning, my smile morphing into a scowl. But the crowd moves like a herd of cattle, oblivious to what's happened.

"Our school uniforms should come with breastplates, right?"

Sam's voice snaps me out of my anger, and I close my locker with a laugh.

"Helmets, at least," I say.

She nudges her chin toward my clenched fist where the locket dangles. "A gift from Henry?"

I bite my lower lip, nervous and a little alarmed. It's only been a few hours since Henry and I first kissed. "News travels fast."

"I may have heard a rumor or two at swim practice this morning."

And suddenly, I wonder if Sam is angry about the news, or if she even believes it at all. I'm anxious about backlash, what people will think. But one glimpse at the sparkle in my friend's eyes, and I know there's nothing malicious about her teasing. "I was going to tell you," I say.

She waves me off like it's no big deal, and relief eases through me. No question Catherine and her friends will hate me, but I need Sam, her friendship, the belief I've got at least one person on my side.

"Do you want me to help you put it on?" Sam says, and holds out her hand. "It's okay, you can let go. I promise not to run away with it, even if I am a bit jealous."

Jealous? "I didn't think Henry was your type."

"Oh, he's not—" She zooms in on the necklace. "Henry puts on a show, pretends he's a typical rich boy. But I've seen him at council meetings. There's more to him than most people realize."

I hand her the locket, turn, and lift my hair. The chain is cool against my skin and the heart thumps against my chest. I clasp my hand around it as I turn.

"Thank you," I say, my voice barely above a whisper. "I'm a klutz when it comes to putting on jewelry." This simple locket is the most expensive thing I've ever worn, and my eyes swim with emotion I can't process.

Through my blurred vision, a trio of girls walk toward me, smirking and pointing.

Too late I realize they're friends of Catherine's. There's no time to turn around, to hide the locket or the look of joy on my face.

"Nice necklace," Liz says, flashing a sinner's sneer. "I think Catherine has one just like it." The three of them pass, cackling.

"Forget them," Sam says with a dismissive wave of her hand. "Forget everything I said before and wear that locket with pride, girl. You deserve it. Hell, you're practically a rock star now."

My throat dries. "More Johnny Rotten than John Lennon," I say, thinking that clearly not everyone will be excited about this turn of events. Has Henry told his friends about me, about us? Are we a couple now?

Sam snorts. "Haters will hate. But you're a symbol of hope." She squeezes my forearm. My body is thirsty, drinking up her encouragement. "I obviously underestimated you. If you can knock Queen Catherine off her pedestal, there's reason to believe in all kinds of miracles."

A rush of satisfaction wells up inside me, a perverse thrill that my developing relationship with Henry has stoked such gut-deep and varying emotions.

"Come on, I'll buy you something to eat," Sam says, and points to my plain paper lunch bag. "I guarantee the infamous fries in the cafeteria taste better than anything you've got in there."

"I don't know," I say, dumping the bag in a trash can as we make our way to the expansive lunchroom, working to ignore the sharp sense of dread that seeps down my neck. "My mother makes a mean cheese sandwich."

Despite Sam's assurances that I should wear my new relationship status like a badge of honor, I stare more at the floor than straight ahead as we make our way to the cafeteria. Sam talks the whole way, loud enough to drown out the hollow echo of my pulse.

My anxiety peaks as we cross the threshold, too late for me to turn around, retrieve my bag lunch from the trash. I lift my head instead.

It's not the greasy smell of fast food that hits me, but rather the crisp scent of fruit and fresh-baked bread. Unlike at my old school, there's no fried chicken on the menu, no slop to pass off as soup.

My eyes widen as I'm handed an overflowing plate of fries after ordering. "I know, right?" Sam says, nodding with approval at my tray. "I'd suggest we share, but that's really against my nature." She pulls her tray up against her chest. "I'm sure you'll manage those on your own."

Catherine's friend Marie slides into line beside me, and I brace for confrontation. "You know what they say," she says, and eyes my lunch. "One moment on the lips, a lifetime on the—" Her hips shift, bump against mine.

She's off and laughing before I can respond. I resist the urge to trade in my fries for greens, but exchange the soda for bottled water. As Sam pays, I scan the room for an open table.

There are a couple of spots beside Liz and Marie. Liz shoots me a sly look and I avert my gaze. I'm so not ready for this.

"Hey, Anne, we've got room," Marie shouts, her lips twisted with amusement. It's more dare than invitation. And I'm now the focal point of sixty-some sets of eyes.

The cafeteria noise grinds to a halt. There's a split second of silence before a few muttered whispers break the hush. Pieces of conversation float through the air.

"Can you believe—?"

"Henry and . . . her?"

"He's crazy."

The gossip bubbles up around me until I can't tell where it's coming from anymore. My chest hurts, as though someone's using me in a bench press—and all I can think of is Henry, how I wish he were here, deflecting, defending, blocking the harsh whispers and accusing stares.

I shake my head, pull myself together, tune out the cacophony of gossip, and follow Sam to a long table dotted with familiar, friendly faces and nonjudgmental looks. A cute boy with spiked hair and ice blue eyes shifts down on the bench to make room for me.

"Hey," he says like I'm not a spectacle, like we're the only table of people in the crowded room. "I loved your reading of *Le Deuxieme Sexe* in English last week. A bold choice."

Sam rolls her eyes. "You'll have to forgive Chris. He's a bit of a geek when it comes to French literature."

"And educated ladies," he says, winking.

"Back off, tiger," Sam says. "Anne is definitely off the market."

I bite into a crispy fry and wash it down with a long gulp of water. I forget about Liz and Marie, focus instead on Sam and Chris, the others gathered around the table talking, teasing, and having fun. Maybe I *can* fit it here. Build a new life. Forget the past.

For a few blissful minutes, I almost believe it.

CHAPTER NINETEEN
Henry

The glass-covered rooftop patio of the London Tower restaurant boasts the best view of Medina. Below, the town is a sprawling kingdom of forest, water, and beach. Houses, even the Tudor mansion, resemble pushpins on a map, fading into the maze of streams, trees, and back roads.

But it's not at all the view I'm checking out.

A strand of hair sticks to Anne's lips. Lips I haven't been able to take my eyes off since the waiter seated us. The way they move when she talks, smiles, laughs—Christ, it's the worst when she laughs.

She tucks her hair behind her ear, tilts her head, and sighs. "It's beautiful here."

I'm speechless.

People often mistake the restaurant for a castle, wedged into the side of a mountain at the end of a narrow tree-lined road. White Christmas lights hang from the branches all year long, giving the impression you're at the entrance of the Enchanted Forest. It's the perfect place to take Anne tonight—exclusive, expensive, and private, with an emphasis on private. I can't get enough of being alone with her.

Our table is tucked in the corner, surrounded by so many flowers, the smell is cloying. Flickering flames from the table-top candles alternate shadow and light across her face, and I'm at once both anxious and thrilled. Anne is the unknown, my Cracker Jack box surprise.

I raise my water in a toast. "To beginnings."

Our glasses clink. Her eyes meet mine.

The waiter sets our plates on the table. The scent of onions and red wine melds with the smell of braised chicken wafting from Anne's dish, something I can't pronounce, French maybe.

"The moon looks huge from up here," she murmurs.

"I've always had a fascination with space," I say.

"Me too. When I was little, I wanted to be an astronaut." I sense her embarrassment and she shrugs. "I saw this movie about space camp, and that was it for me."

It's rare for her to open up. I lean in close. "And then?"

Anne sighs. "I realized how much science I'd need to learn—not my best subject. By the time I hit middle school, I'd flipped through a dozen or more career options. English teacher. Dancer." She cuts into her chicken, takes a bite.

My eyes follow her lips again as she chews, swallows, moans. I was wrong before. It's the worst when she moans.

"I also wanted to be a chef," she says, and her eyes go all dreamy. "To be able to cook like this . . ."

My wild boar looks bland and pale in comparison to Anne's dish, and my stomach is too twisted for food. I force down a forkful anyway. "What stopped you?"

Her expression darkens and she looks away. "I worked at a fast food joint for a few weeks." Anne pushes her food to the opposite side of the plate and holds the fork there, thinking. She glances up at me, expression heavy. "After my dad left, things got tough."

I get it. But while Anne has seemed hesitant about life with her new stepdad, I kind of wish my mom would just chill out and meet someone else, get remarried even. Find a new purpose instead of clinging to the past. I'm almost jealous Anne has a second chance at a real family.

"I'm sorry," I say, but the words seem inadequate.

"What about you?" Anne says. She slices off another piece of chicken. Stabs it with her fork and holds it out, a silent invitation for me to taste.

I allow her to feed me, my heart pulsing so hard I'm surprised it hasn't popped right out of my skin. "Delicious."

Anne folds her hands on top of the table and tilts her head. "So . . ." At my vacant stare, she laughs. "Did you always want a career in politics?"

I cough. "Fuck no." I spear a piece of asparagus, fold it over my fork, and stuff it into my mouth. Chew. Gather my thoughts. "It runs in my blood, though. My grandfather was a senator. Dad, too. Primed for the presidency, some say. And then Arthur. Well, we all know that story."

"Not really. You never mention him," she says. "Or what happened."

A knot forms in my chest. Even before he died, talking about my brother had never been easy.

"Years ago, my grandfather started this tradition, a charity hike up the face of Gander Mountain," I say. "My dad never supported it, thought there were easier ways of giving back to the community. I guess he got real good at writing checks."

I pause to take a sip of water, let the words gather. Anne reaches across the table and covers my hand with hers. Her touch gives me the motivation to keep talking. "When my grandfather died, I restarted the tradition. Dad still wrote checks, but my grandfather loved nature and I wanted to keep his spirit alive."

"That's nice," Anne says. She rubs her thumb across the top of my hand, distracting me from the memories I'm dredging up.

"I ditched out on the last year's hike." I drop my gaze to avoid eye contact. "Went on a date instead." Looking back makes me feel more like an ass. I barely even remember the girl's name. "Even though I'd made a commitment to be there."

Anne nods.

I clear my throat, pull away my hand. "So big brother came to the rescue. It had become a regular occurrence, him saving my ass."

The rest of the story hangs on the tip of my tongue. Arthur wasn't much of an outdoorsman, hadn't spent his younger years exploring the paths, navigating the cliffs. He shouldn't have been in the lead—but Tudor men don't belong at the back of the pack. I look away from Anne, hesitant to tell her the rest.

"We had a lot of rain that year. It wasn't safe." I rush through the rest. "He slipped on a rock and went over the edge. . . . It should have been me."

Anne shakes her head. "That isn't true."

I appreciate her sympathy, maybe even crave it, but she's dead wrong. Arthur never should have been on that hike. And after he died, everything changed.

"So now you're expected to follow in your father's foot-steps? Do what Arthur—"

Couldn't.

I poke around at the food on my plate. "Yeah."

"You seem to hate it, though," she says. "Why not try something else?"

The question jabs at me, makes me squirm. Maybe I could have stood my ground, challenged my father's will, left the politics behind and pursued my dreams. In time I might have even been able to let go of the guilt. But one look at the hope, the *desperation* in my mother's eyes and—fighting it felt like a lost cause.

"I guess I never thought I had a choice."

Anne raises her glass, her eyebrow. I lean across the table and stop any more questions with a light kiss, terrified she'll ask if I'm okay, scared I'll have to admit that I'm not.

"It's not as bad as it seems," I say, working up a smile. "There are certainly worse career options."

"Except you're not following your passion, Henry."

Her words slice through my insides like a hot knife. I blink. "You can't possibly understand."

Anne sits upright, her muscles rigid, voice tense. "Then explain it. What if you weren't expected to be just like your dad? What would you do? What would you *want* to do?"

"*What if* is a dangerous sport," I say. Our eyes meet and we both know it's the game we've been playing since we first met. "Besides, it's not like I can just drop it now. I live in a different world, Anne."

"Bullshit."

My stomach does a slow roll, tensing up at the direction this conversation is heading.

"Why would you even want to be a politician? I have a hard time respecting a bunch of assholes stepping over the poor to make themselves richer." Her eyes flash, but behind the anger, there's something else.

I open my mouth to interject—this isn't how the night's supposed to go—but Anne silences me with her eyes. She pushes aside her empty plate with disgust. "Do you know what it's like living in a dump, Henry? A place where you become immune to the smell of shit because it's better than asking for help from your creepy-ass landlord?"

Anne's shoulders stiffen, her whole body tenses with rage, with passion.

"No, I don't suppose you would," she says.

"That's harsh," I say, prepared to debate the finer details of our national budget. "Do I think finances could be handled better? Absolutely." I fold my napkin into a tiny square and tuck it under my mostly untouched plate. "Don't you think this is an overreaction, though?"

"You've never experienced . . . poverty," Anne counters. "Money corrupts people. All people. But politicians especially."

I resist the urge to remind her I'll be one of them someday. "That's a very broad brushstroke you're painting with."

She folds her arms across her chest, pale skin nearly translucent against a dress so plum it's almost black. She averts her gaze, bites her lower lip. Even in the throes of her anger, I can't take my eyes off those damn lips. "How can you deny all of the perks and freebies you get?"

I quirk an eyebrow. This is starting to feel like an inquisition.

She picks up her fork and pokes at the empty plate. A steady scratch of steel against porcelain grates on my eardrums, my nerves.

A flush of red creeps up along her neck. Maybe I'm an idiot or something, but I can't figure out what's got her so worked up. My instinct is to give her a hard time, try to lighten the mood. "Hoarding a few misdemeanors, Ms. Boleyn?"

Too late, I realize I've mocked her.

"I'm glad you're amused," she says and tosses her napkin on the table. "But I bet you didn't even have to make a reservation at this restaurant. If I'd come here with someone else, we'd still be outside in line."

The thought of her being on a date with someone else makes my stomach churn.

I reach across the table for her hand but she pulls back. "Anne, I—" My heart settles at the bottom of my rib cage and I fold my hands in my lap, unsure of what to do with them, yearning to touch her, console her, even though I don't really know what's wrong.

A heavy silence hangs between us. I play back our conversation, try to figure out how we got on this track, how I've hurt, offended, *insulted* her. And that's when it hits me, *whollops* me right in the gut. She's right. I *don't* know what it's like to grow up without money and privilege and possessions. Have never worried about a roof over my head or not being able to pay for college.

I tilt my head back, close my eyes. "I'm an asshole."

She doesn't deny it, but the corner of her mouth tilts up.

"Maybe just a jerk," she says. "And I guess I'm a bit of a hypocrite, because ever since my mom married Thomas, I've received some"—she looks at me through hooded lashes—"perks too."

Her words spark something in me—but I can't put my finger on it. A feeling, a purpose, something unexplainable and . . . freeing.

In our moment of shared silence, the music starts. It spills onto the balcony and fills the air. I stand, hold out my arm. Anne hesitates, then fits her small hand into mine. My throat swells as I lead her to the dance floor, curl her into my chest.

A soft purr travels the length of her throat.

I kiss her forehead, the tip of her nose. I'm drunk on her power, mesmerized, and I'm spinning out of control.

Anne stands on her tiptoes, wraps her arms around my neck, and rests her forehead against mine. She presses her mouth to my cheek, my jaw.

Our lips touch.

I pull her tight and the feelings I've suppressed uncoil and thrash inside me.

I taste her.

Breathe her. Feel her.

Only her.

"What have you done to me?" I whisper.

CHAPTER TWENTY

Anne

I stretch out on the blanket, pull my hoodie over my ears, and prop myself up on my elbows. Late afternoon sunlight reflects off the white page of my history text, further blurring the words, my focus.

"I've gone over this so many times, I think I've fallen *into* the Great Depression," I say. "Nothing is sticking. I'm going to flunk Ms. McLaughlin's test, for sure."

Sam rolls onto her side. "Who the hell brings their homework to the beach?"

"Someone who actually wants to pass Ms. McLaughlin's test tomorrow?" I squint at her through my sunglasses. Despite the sun, there's a seasonal chill in the air. Goose bumps pepper her bare arms and legs. "You're questioning my sanity when you're out here in shorts and a thin T-shirt? I can see your nipples." She smirks and I add, "Let's grab a coffee."

Her gaze lifts over my shoulder and I know without looking what she sees, the reason we're sprawled out on the damp sand, shivering in the lackluster autumn sun.

"Forget that. Things are just starting to heat up around here," she says with a blush.

I roll over so I can check out the action too. A crowd gathers around four guys in swim trunks playing a sweaty game of volleyball. Bile creeps along my throat as John's torso extends to meet the ball midair. He drives it over the net, straight at Charles.

Sam sucks in a gasp.

Charles takes the dive—misses. The smirk on John's face sends a tremor of disgust along my core. He slaps Rick in a high five, and then falls back to take the serve.

"John's such a creep," I say.

Sam lifts her sunglasses onto the top of her head and sits up, folds her legs into a pretzel. Reaching back, she pulls her hair into a loose ponytail and sighs. "He's certainly no prince."

I sit up and dust off my textbook, tuck it into my bag. "Whatever. Fairy tales are overrated anyway."

Sam scoffs. "Ironic, since you're living one now."

My stomach twists. Despite Sam's early support of my relationship with Henry, an occasional snide remark slips out, a hint of jealousy or something . . . more, something raw and honest, uncomfortable even. "No, seriously. I don't believe in Happily Ever After."

Being with Henry has given me the courage to move on from the past, to let go of some of my guilt and shame. It's freeing, but I'm not naive. There's no such thing as forever.

"Yeah, I get it. Your life has been so rough."

I flinch as though burned. "Low blow. You say that and don't even know me."

"How can I? You never talk about yourself," she snaps.

Sam grabs my wrist. I stare at it, take a few calming breaths, and then look up to meet her gaze. Where the hell is this coming from?

"I'm sorry," she says. "That wasn't fair."

I chew on the inside of my cheek. "It's okay. I'm just not real great with—"

"Girlfriends," she says, and grins, like she's filled in the blanks, has got me all figured out. Maybe she does.

"Look, I get it," she says. "This place can feel like a prison. Making friends is tough." She leans forward and presses her hands on either side of my cheeks, forcing me to stare at her. "You know everything about me—and I feel like I know nothing about you. I'm not asking for you to tap a vein here, just let me in a little. Friends share things."

"There's not much to tell," I say, pulling out of her grip. Her handprints leave warm tingles on my skin.

"Bullshit," she says, laughing. "What about ex-boyfriends? Your old school? I want the dirt. A girl like you has to have secrets."

My cell phone chirps and I look down at the text, eager for a distraction. These topics are taboo, off limits, sealed in a vault.

"Was that Henry?"

I look up and nod, warmth spreading through my body. He's on his way to the beach to pick me up, an impromptu date.

"Trust your knight in shining armor to save you from deep conversation," she says.

"I told you, I don't believe in fairy tales."

Sam arches an eyebrow. "How about knights on white stallions?"

"Funny," I say.

When she doesn't laugh, I whip my head around. Holy shit. Sam's not joking. Henry straddles an enormous horse, loitering at the edge of the beach and watching his friends play volleyball. A couple of girls hover around him, stroking the animal's long mane and ogling my boyfriend.

My boyfriend.

"Is that allowed?" I say, my voice filled with such wonder even I'm embarrassed.

Sam shrugs. "He's a Tudor."

As if that should explain everything.

Henry watches the game a few seconds more, stealing glances at his cell, scanning the beach, looking for—

Me.

I fire off a quick text: *I see you.*

Henry checks his phone, lifts his head, and looks our way. He waves when he spots me, sending a delicious shiver along the nape of my neck. I begin to stand, but Sam grabs my wrist, holds on like she's afraid I'll leave. Her eyes cloud with concern. "Promise me we'll talk about this again?"

She's right—if I'm ever going to fit in and find my place in this town, I need to start opening up. "I promise. And I do appreciate your concern. Honest."

The soft whinny of Henry's horse alerts me to his arrival, and I turn, unprepared for the way my heart speeds up at the sight of him.

"Something wrong with your Audi?"

He raises his eyebrow. "Figured we could slow things down a bit today."

The double meaning isn't lost on me—or Sam, who whistles low and playfully, reminding us she's there.

"Bacon could use a run."

"You call your horse Bacon?" Sam says, tilting her head with disbelief. Henry presses his lips together, and I can't tell if he's joking.

"Hey, Sam," Henry says. "Mind if I steal your friend for a few hours?"

"Like I have any choice in the matter," she says, and sticks out her tongue.

There's something so girlish about her, so innocent and

naive. In my skeleton-imprinted hoodie I must look like the bad influence, the troublemaker. I'm struck by our differences, how it must be true that opposites attract, and when I look up at Henry, the feeling intensifies.

Henry holds out his hand and my blood freezes.

"You don't expect me to get on that thing, do you?" I say.

The horse chuffs as if I've offended him. Snorts. Nuzzles up against Sam.

Henry's expression darkens, and for a second I think he's upset, annoyed that I'm a chicken, that I've ruined his surprise. "I've never been on a horse before," I admit.

Henry pumps his eyebrows—twice. This is so corny, *he* is so corny, but damn if I'm not laughing, giving in to his invitation. "You're not really scared, are you?" he says.

Challenge accepted.

Henry guides me through the steps: one hand on the horse's shoulder, one toe in the stirrup, I bounce, propel myself up and over the saddle, shuffle my back into Henry's chest as he wraps his arms tight around my waist and gathers the reigns. His breath is hot in my ear. "See, that wasn't bad."

My heart thumps so fast, it's like a drumbeat accompaniment to his voice.

"Have fun, kids," Sam says as we trot away from the beach toward the thickly wooded forest surrounding the semiprivate cove of sand. A chorus of voices taunts us and teases, fires shots at my back. Henry's oblivious, or doesn't care—either way, I'm envious of his ability to deflect.

We move onto a well-worn path and the horse's hooves crunch over the fallen leaves, the scent of evergreen blowing across my face with each of his long strides. Overhead, sun cuts swaths of light through the shadows.

I grip the animal's white mane so tight my knuckles appear translucent. In spite of my fear, I'm captivated.

"You *are* taking me to your serial killer cabin in the woods," I say.

Henry nestles his mouth on the nape of my neck, his lips cool and wet. "Believe me, murder is the last thing on my mind."

I try to breathe, but it's like someone's hands are gripping my lungs, squeezing them tight. The deeper we go into the woods, the more anxious, nervous, excited I become. I focus on the path, on how Henry commands the horse with a subtle tug on the reins, how it seems to know just where to go, what curve of the path to follow.

"It's a bit cheesy," I say, teasing. "This whole horseback riding trick. A little over the top, even for you."

Henry chuckles. "The Tudor stables aren't far from here," he says. "Bacon needed a run anyway. I thought it might get your attention."

I think about the crowd gathered on the shore, watching Henry, his horse, the two of us riding off together, and I swallow the unease. Maybe his friends are used it, but I don't like being in the spotlight. "It got everyone's attention."

He nuzzles his cheek against my neck. "Yours is all that matters."

Through the pocket of trees, a meadow unfolds at the crest of a small stream. An open wicker basket rests on a bright red sleeping bag at the center of the patchy grass. A single rose springs from a tall vase resting between two empty wine glasses. It's all I can do to stop the tremble in my voice as I try to remain nonchalant.

"Premeditated romance?"

He squeezes my waist and the horse comes to a stop. "I wanted—needed—time alone with you," he says in that low, gravely tone that turns my insides out.

Henry helps me to the ground and motions for me to sit while he ties the horse's reins to a tree. The animal dips its head into the stream, extending its long tongue into the water.

Henry reaches into the basket and pulls out a bottle of wine, pours us each a glass, holds his up to offer a toast. "To us," he says. For the first time, I notice the light freckles under the corner of his right eye.

The pterodactyl wings smash against my rib cage and I blink to slow down the tears. No one has ever been so nice to me, treated me with such care, and I realize with a shuddering terror that if ever I believed in forever, in Happily Ever After, it might be right now.

"It's been a tough few days," he says, setting his glass on the blanket. He reaches into the basket and produces a strawberry dipped in chocolate. I remember the first night we met and try not to taint this moment with thoughts of John. "I couldn't wait another minute to see you."

I chew on my bottom lip. "Didn't you have football practice or something this afternoon?"

Henry shrugs. "Probably." He lifts the strawberry to my mouth. I part my lips. My whole body tingles with anticipation. "I'm having trouble focusing on anything but—"

"Us," I say, and take a bite.

Chocolate sticks to the corner of my mouth and I lick it away. I'm on fire, burning up with expectation and wanting. I lean, crash into him. Our tongues find each other and tangle into knots.

A subtle shift and I'm flat on my back, Henry's body hovering over mine.

"I can't get enough of you," he says.

I breathe out an inaudible response and arch my back, an invitation. But Henry pulls away. He sits upright and runs his hand through his hair, mutters a curse. "I'm sorry."

"Too soon," I say, breathless and scared. It's more of a question than a statement—I don't want him to stop.

He chuckles without humor. "Jesus, Anne. I can't control myself when I'm with you."

"Is that so bad?" I say, sliding into sitting position.

Henry stares off into the distance and I'd do anything to know what he's thinking, feeling. "My mother doesn't approve."

"Neither do your friends," I say quietly. I'm not surprised by the admission—I'm just not sure what it means for us. A seed of doubt roots itself in my gut.

"They don't know you," Henry says, reaching for my hand. He rubs his thumb absently over my flesh. My skin tingles where he touches it. "If they just took the time to—"

I press my finger to his lips.

"We both know it wouldn't change anything if they did." Sam's words echo in my subconscious, rendering me vulnerable. If I want to fit in here, keep Henry, give *us* a chance, I have to confide in him. Yet, I can't bring myself to find the words.

Henry drops his head and sighs. "No, it wouldn't matter. My mom's stubborn." He falls so he's flat on his back and motions for me to lie next to him, pulling me in to his chest.

"Protective," I counter.

"Maybe I'm just a stereotype," he says. "Rich kid whose parents were never really around. The guy who eventually goes off the deep end and—"

Hooks up with someone like me?

I clear my throat. "I don't believe that."

His face turns more somber. I bury my head deeper into his arms and he squeezes me close. "I don't know. I've made some pretty stupid mistakes."

"Haven't we all?"

Henry shifts a little, and I untangle myself from his arms. He props up on one elbow, so that I'm facing him, and focuses on the overhead clouds dotting the endless sky. Then he turns and gives me a lopsided grin. "I don't know. You're pretty perfect."

Henry's words hit me in the middle of my chest. He doesn't realize how wrong he is, how I'm so far from perfect that maybe his mother and his friends have a reason not to trust me, to believe I'm not right for him. Tears well in the corner of my eyes.

"Oh, hey, don't cry," he says. "I don't care what anyone else thinks. It can't change how I feel about you. You're everything I want."

"And if I'm not?"

He thumbs away a tear. "What's really going on here, Anne?"

The words come out in a rush. "I've hurt people," I say. "People I love."

He reaches for my hand. "Shit, who hasn't? Sometimes it's the people closest to us we hurt the most."

A pained squeak escapes my lips. "But it shouldn't be like that." I'm really crying now, my cheeks streaked and wet.

"Anne, tell me. What happened? What is it?"

"I'm so fucking stupid, Henry." My shoulders shake from sobbing. Everything hurts. "My sister caught me with her boyfriend."

CHAPTER TWENTY-ONE
Henry

My body tenses as I take in Anne's words.

"You have a *sister*?"

I play back conversations, look for actions and clues, some indication that Anne isn't an only child, that maybe she's told me this important life fact before.

She shifts, presses her body flatter against mine. I don't move out of reach, but my blood cools under the waning sunlight. Anne has a sister. Jesus. What else hasn't she told me?

"Her name is Mary," she says, in a voice so quiet I have to strain to hear the words. "She's a couple of years older."

I mull this over and wait for her to continue. Maybe I'm overthinking it, but I don't understand how I couldn't have known, how I've never heard her—or her mother—talk about an older sibling. Not even a whisper.

"Is she in college?" I say, because it's clear Anne needs prodding.

She pushes herself upright and sits cross-legged at my side. I roll over to face her, wanting—expecting—more.

"Well, she's in a . . . hospital," Anne says.

The quiver of her lower lip transforms my anger and confusion into worry. I reach over and take her hand. "Is she sick?"

Anne laughs without humor. "That's one way of putting it."

With her free hand, she pinches off a blade of grass, drops it on the blanket, and flicks it aside. Repeats until there's a small pile. "Mary is in the psychiatric ward," she says, and pulls away. She rubs at her wrist and my eyes are drawn to the pale, unmarked flesh there. "The doctors think she's depressed. Suicidal." Her voice softens. "They say she's certifiable."

I sit upright and pull her close. She doesn't resist, but twists so that her back is against my chest. With my arms wrapped around her, her heart thumps wildly against mine.

"Mary's always been unstable," Anne says. "Even when we were little." She inhales, like she's trying to stop the waver of her voice. "We thought she was getting better—had her shit under control. But then, Dad left Mom and—" Anne pauses.

"She fell apart?" I fill in.

Anne interlaces her fingers through mine. "I'm the one who lost it," she says. "I did stupid things—skipped school, started fights, got tangled up with the wrong crowd."

"I get it," I say, squeezing her with assurance, for comfort, but all I really want is to get back to the part about her sister's boyfriend. "You needed to *feel* something. I've been there."

I almost can't get the words out though, because I'm picturing another man's hands on Anne's body.

She slides out of my embrace and pushes herself up, starts gathering the empty glasses, the food, the picnic basket. Like hell she's getting off that easy.

I stand and grab Anne's shoulders, force her to look me in the eye. Her lips are chapped, skin pale. It's like she's dying, dead, already a ghost. I hate that this is tearing her up, but our relationship can't survive if she isn't honest. If I can't understand *what* led her to such a betrayal.

I lean forward to kiss the corner of her mouth, taste salt. "Mary was unstable—you said it yourself. Her depression wasn't your fault," I say.

Anne closes her eyes. "I used to be so damned jealous of her when we were kids," she says, her voice thick with emotion. "My parents doted on her. Did everything for her. It got worse after her diagnosis; it's like she couldn't do anything wrong."

She stares over me, through me. "We fought. Stupid sister stuff, at first. She'd nag at me for doing pot, always letting me know how disappointed she was in me—and I'd respond by smoking up in front of her. Just to piss her off. Things escalated fast from there. The more she bitched, the more spiteful I got. It was like I was . . ." Anne eases away from me and shakes her head.

I can feel it in my gut, the anguish, her guilt. . . .

"Possessed," she finally says. Fresh tears form in the corners of her eyes. "I don't know how else to explain it. I *wanted* to hurt her. Like seeing her in pain might take some of mine away." She holds onto the back of her neck with both hands. "How fucked up is that? I knew she was going crazy and I didn't stop. We'd lost our dad to his affair, and because of my actions, we were losing each other, too."

"Everyone deals with grief in their own way," I say. "I know it sucks, but you're not the reason she's in the hospital."

"Wrong again." Anne looks up and her eyes shimmer. "Mary was only looking out for me, trying to get me back on track. At first, it seemed like that's what her boyfriend wanted too."

Another bout of jealousy rocks through me. Suddenly I'm unable to process anything but another guy kissing her . . . touching her. I know it's selfish, that this isn't about me, but I can't stop visualizing him, her, the two of them. . . . "I don't get it," I say, choking back anger. "You were so mad at her—at them—for *helping* you that you . . . had sex with her boyfriend?"

"We didn't actually have *sex*," Anne says, and a tear crawls down her cheek. "Mary thinks that's what happened, though—lots of people do. Maybe if I'd been a weaker person, Jesse could have gotten his way. He sure as hell tried."

Another tear slides down her cheek and she hangs her head before I can wipe it away.

"I guess it started out innocent enough—little things I mistook for kindness. Like he was just trying to make a good impression on Mary's family. And I enjoyed the attention." She blushes. "Not in *that* way. I mean, after dating a string of guys who cared more about their bongs than me, it was easy to get caught up in . . . normal. Or what I thought was normal."

Anne takes a deep breath. Exhales. "Mary loved seeing us hang out. Said it made her heart happy to have the two most important people in her life getting along. It seemed to even cover up the sibling crap going on between us."

I reach for her, but she doesn't give in. I've never felt more helpless.

"A few months later, though, things started to change," she says. "Or maybe I just became more aware. Jesse was always around, consoling, taking over as the *man of the house*. His subtle flirtations became more overt."

Sensing what comes next, the cracks in my heart give way a little as I absorb Anne's pain. This time, when I draw her close, she doesn't push me away.

"The more aggressive Jesse became, the more I realized he wasn't at all who I thought he was," she says. "But how could I tell my sister that? She loved him. I put up with it for a while—spent more time away from home, got myself deeper in shit," she says. "I should have realized my rejection was pissing him off."

She exhales with a shudder that vibrates through her entire body.

"I came home drunk one night, and never made it up to bed. I'd stripped out of my clothes—they stank like smoke and beer—and curled up on the couch. I thought I was alone," she says. "When Mary came downstairs in the morning, Jesse and I were entangled on the couch—barely dressed. I don't even know when he slid under the blanket. He knew Mary would find us like that. A sick and twisted way to get back at me for rejecting him."

Before I can react, she turns her eyes to me. The dark pools draw me in like quicksand. "It didn't look good, I know that," she says. "But I never had sex with Jesse. No matter how crappy I was feeling, I would never cross that line."

She kicks at a rock. Sends it flying into the creek with a light splash. "What I didn't know was that Jesse had started planting thoughts in my sister's head, making her think I was trying to break them up. God knows what other bullshit he was feeding her. He told her I took advantage of him that night."

"Because he was so fucking weak?" I snap. Christ, this guy's an asshole. "He set you up." Every piece of me wants to find this shithead and pile drive him into the ground. "But why let him win? Why let everyone think the worst of you?"

"Jesse was Mr. Perfect around anyone else. While I was busy making a reputation for myself, Jesse was scoring brownie points with my mom and Mary. They thought the guy was an Adonis. Probably still do." Anne shakes her head. "Sometimes, it's just easier not to fight, you know?"

Her words hit home.

"After Mary was committed, Mom met Thomas and next thing I know, we're riding off in his limo with the promise of a fresh start," she says. "Thomas has set her up in the best hospital money can buy—no way we could have afforded it. But even if we had access to the same care here, Mary would have stayed away. She hates me. And now, I'm somehow supposed to forget. Simple, right?" She sighs. "I guess that's why I confronted John that first night. I didn't know what people knew, or thought they knew. I'd been too subtle with Jesse— and there was no way in hell I'd make that mistake again."

Her shoulders slump, and her eyes fade to dull charcoal. It almost kills me to see her pain.

"I don't know how to forgive myself, how to let it go. If only I'd told her sooner what was happening, maybe . . ." She reaches up and touches my cheek.

My chest swells so full I think it might split in half.

"I have a history of fucking things up when the going gets tough. And that scares me, Henry. Because you're right. This—us—is never going to be easy."

CHAPTER TWENTY-TWO

Anne

I pause in front of the glamorous master suite and brace for whatever version of my mother I will find. The anxious woman, nervous about fitting in, terrified of losing all of . . . this? Or some semblance of the woman I remember—the confident, nurturing mother who isn't afraid to admit a piece of her misses our old life, our old selves.

My father.

And yes, Mary.

Before Dad left, we didn't walk on diamond-crusted eggshells. Mom didn't wear high heels to the grocery store. *We* didn't keep secrets. Confiding in her used to be—

Easy.

My mother emerges from her dressing room, luminous in her aqua ball gown, hair pinned up and curly. Her heart-shaped face glows in the incandescent light.

"Hello, dear," she says when she sees me. "You look

different. . . . Worried, maybe." She pauses to collect her thoughts. "Is everything okay?"

Things between us are less strained now that we've moved away from my mistakes, her heartache . . . Mary. But part of me knows she's worried I'm going to somehow fuck this up. Her eyes narrow as she studies me, tries to assess the situation, determine what's wrong. Whether I've got good news, or if I'm in trouble at school, or maybe I'm knocked up. She always thinks the worst of me. In addition to committing my sister to the psych ward, I'm also somehow to blame for Dad running off with that librarian.

My mother's voice lifts, her skin pales. "Anne? What is it?"

"It's not bad," I say, and blink, blink, blink away the tears and the fears. I move over to the bed, unfold my body onto the cream-colored duvet sprinkled with tiny pink roses.

My mother sits on the edge and tilts her body so she's facing me. "It's not your father, is it?"

I shake my head, struggle not to frown. Why would she think that after all this time, my father would call, that he'd even want a relationship with . . . me, the problem daughter? I wonder whether he's visited my sister, or if she's met his new wife.

My mother's shoulders sink, weighed down with relief. She pats my leg. "That's good. I worry he'll try to contact you now that—"

Now that we have money.

"It's not about Dad," I interrupt, biting back a knee-jerk *he's-not-like-that* response. He didn't leave my mother for money.

My mother frets, her fingers twisting at her shiny new diamond-studded wedding band. "Good, because I want this to work, for you to be happy here."

"I *am* happy," I say. I'm totally blushing now, and if she knows me, remembers who I am, who I was before Dad shattered our illusions of happiness and true love and forever, she'll see I'm telling the truth.

"You've started to make friends, then?" my mother says, nodding. Her eyes shine with hope. "Some nice girls from the area?" She stands, busying herself with getting ready for the unknown checkmark on her social calendar.

This evening's gown spills over her hips, flows onto the floor, forms a satin puddle on the white carpet. She sits at the dressing table and rummages through her jewelry box, holds diamonds, topaz, and pearls up against her ears and neck.

I wait for her to notice me in the reflection.

Our eyes meet. I force myself not to blink and she freezes midmotion, the string of pearls clutched in her fingers.

Her voice is low and soft, barely more than a whisper. "What is it, ladybug?"

"I've met someone," I finally say.

My mother's expression is an eerie mixture of confusion and joy and fear rolled into one giant wrecking ball. Only her lips move. "You're dating someone?"

I grin, afraid my face will crack, relieved and scared. It's more than just dating, but I doubt she'd understand. "Yep. And I'm going to see him again tonight."

"Someone from . . . Medina?"

I nod.

She blows out a breath that is more than relief. I don't need to read her mind to know what she is thinking. She's wondering who, and how, and maybe why, but most of all she's wondering when, because she knows, or thinks she knows, that when we left I'd sworn off relationships altogether. A twinge of something akin to pain skips across my chest, and I don't know if it's because I'm broken or missing or maybe even that I'm healing, almost healed.

My mother twists on the stool so that she's looking at me, really looking. Her smile is genuine, so wide I could count all her teeth if I wanted.

"Come on, ladybug, spill," she says, and she's suddenly standing, practically running toward me, taking me back, back, back to my childhood, to days when we laughed and played. Before Mary got sick. Before Dad left. She sits on the edge of the bed and pokes my thigh with a long manicured finger. "Who is it?"

I giggle—and almost gasp, because the sound is so unnatural for me. I can't remember when it happened last and so I do it again as she jabs and jabs at my leg, poking and prodding me to share my secrets, to confess.

"Don't make me tickle it out of you," my mother says.

Before I can protest, she tackles me, her fingers expertly navigating their way under my T-shirt and into my armpits.

A strand of her perfectly placed hair swings loose, sticks to the side of her lip. She's fast becoming a hot mess, but it's like she doesn't care, because for this moment, we're back to who we once were. Not just mother and daughter, but best friends, the kind that whisper and share secrets, laugh together, cry together.

Survive together.

My mother is beautiful when she's real like this.

"Who is it?" she says through gritted teeth, and at last, I relent.

"Henry," I say, kind of breathless.

She freezes as though I've slapped her. I can hear the gears working, the *click-clank-clunk* as she tries to process, to understand how this could have happened.

"The Tudor boy?" she finally says.

"He broke up with Catherine," I say so fast, knowing that's the question she's thinking, wondering. "For real. I didn't ask him to." My body tenses in defense. "I've really fallen for him, Mom."

The realization shocks me, makes my whole body quiver.

Because I know it's true—and that as ridiculous as it seems, as unrealistic as it is, I think Henry's falling for me, too.

My mother's hands come together with a loud clap. "Anne, this is fantastic news." She pats the edge of the bed, beckons me to come closer, and turns her body in to mine so we're face-to-face, the way roommates or best friends sit to gossip. "Well done, ladybug! We must tell Thomas right away."

My blood turns to ice.

Well done?

"Thomas?" My voice is so tiny, barely more than a squeak. I wait for her to reverse, to tell me first that she's happy for me, to ask for more details, pause for that *tell-me-more* moment. A cool chill seeps into my bones. "Why would Thomas . . . care?"

Her voice drops to a whisper. "The Tudors are the most influential family in Medina, Anne. Maybe the whole state." She leans closer. "Thomas has bid to do the architectural plans on a number of projects owned by the Tudors. If you're dating their son, he's practically a shoo-in—"

My body vibrates. "You want to use my relationship as leverage?" The bitter taste of bile crawls up my throat.

She stares at me with disbelief and presses her hand against her chest. "Really, Anne. Aren't you being dramatic?"

"After everything we've been through. You're actually serious right now?"

"Ladybug," she says, tentative and nervous. "I'm surprised by this reaction. You know we are ecstatic for you. What's really going on here? Don't you like Thomas?"

"This isn't about Thomas," I say so slow my voice slurs. "It's about me. Your daughter. How I *feel*."

She stands and makes her way back to the dressing table, lifts a string of pearls and holds them up to her neck. "After what happened back home, I'm thrilled you've met someone," she says, though her words are thick with dual meaning. "And all the more thrilled it's Henry Tudor; he's quite the catch. Now, would you help me with this clasp?"

I cross the floor to her, pull the necklace tight around her neck, and fasten the lock, fingers trembling.

She lifts her hand, entwines her fingers with mine. "The real test, ladybug, is keeping things interesting," she says. "A boy like Henry Tudor is easily bored."

I open my mouth to tell her she's wrong, that Henry isn't like Dad. Henry is handsome and popular, and all the girls want him—but he's not a player.

The words don't come out. I study my mother's reflection in the mirror, look really hard. The wrinkles around her eyes are gone, her skin radiant and smooth. Thomas's house is filled with sparkling, shiny things, material goods that light up my mother's eyes. And for the first time since we've moved to Medina, I realize, there is no going back.

"I know you won't believe this," she says, "but I truly want you to be happy. I *am* happy for you. Young love *should* be like this. Not dangerous and deceitful. I trust you, Anne. I believe you've learned from the past."

Her words slam into me with the force of a hurricane and I am suddenly at a loss for words. So shocked I can't scream, can't cry, can hardly open my mouth. Because it's clear now she doesn't believe me, that despite everything she's told me, the assurances, the forgiveness, she actually thinks I slept with Jesse, that I'm capable of such a horrible betrayal.

My stomach churns.

How can I have a fresh start—move on and forget the past—when even my mother, my own flesh and blood—doesn't believe in me?

CHAPTER TWENTY-THREE

Henry

Anne's different tonight.

Manic, not romantic. Her smile is wide, but it's a little off, maybe forced. She's more Hyde than Jekyll. I can't quite put my finger on it.

I shift on my feet, change position, tuck the helmet under my armpit and run a hand through my hair. "You're acting weird. Did the talk with your mom not go well?"

I've been so wrapped up in making amends with my own mother, trying hard to follow her rules and show her that nothing has changed, I never stopped to consider that Mrs. Harris might not approve of . . . me.

Anne raises one eyebrow. "Are you going to stand there and gawk or hop on?" she says, and revs Clarice's engine.

Maybe I'm imagining it, but a flash of something like hurt trips across her eyes and then fades. I hesitate before reaching for her shoulder. "I thought we agreed not to keep secrets."

Anne throws back her head like she's exasperated. "I just need to let loose. Have some fun."

She shifts forward, making room for me on the back of her bike. Giving in, I slip on the helmet, slide in behind her, and grip the back handrail. The cool metal bites at my skin. She guns the throttle and Clarice's roar reverberates across the lake.

I lean forward and wrap my hands around her waist. Her heartbeat presses against my palms. Erratic. Too fast. I can't tell whether she's frightened or confused.

I nuzzle up to her neck, whisper in her ear. "Hit it, babe." Clarice lurches forward. Anne weaves around the stretch of speed bumps on my driveway and we sway back and forth, our movements in sync. Those speed bumps seem silly now, but as kids, Arthur and I would race our soapbox cars along the pavement. My mother always worried we'd crash, or worse, be hit by one of Dad's never-ending string of visitors.

A sigh settles at the back of my throat. That's the kind of stuff I miss, what's been absent for the past year. It's like my mother's nurturing feeling just got up and left, a sad side effect of losing the two people she loved most in this world.

I shake away the memories and focus on the present. My future. Not all of the pieces have clicked into place, but there's no question Anne will be part of it—part of me. She's the first person I think about in the morning, her eyes the last image I see before I fall asleep. In the end, it doesn't matter who approves. Not my mother, not even my friends. But I want to believe they'll come around.

As we hit the main road, Anne gives the throttle some gas and we pick up speed. The wind flicks my visor like a whip. I press my head against her back and shut my eyes, sucked in by how effortlessly Anne commands the bike.

I guess it's normal that things feel a little awkward and foreign tonight. This is still new. *We* are still new.

Complicated.

I open my eyes just as Anne turns on to a side street and guides Clarice down a lonely back alley. The strip mall is closed for the night, lights off, doors buttoned up tight. The dumpsters overflow with recycling and garbage that will be emptied by morning.

Anne weaves right. Then left. Turns on to another abandoned street. It ends just up ahead, but we don't stop and the bike easily slides from the asphalt to a narrow gravel path that leads to the train tracks.

"How the hell do you know about this place?" I say, sitting upright. Rocks, twigs, and leaves crunch, crackle, and snap under Clarice's tires.

"I know everything," she says.

Her voice is almost a yell over the noise of Clarice's growl, but it's laced with carefree amusement, and I smile despite the peculiar sensation building in my gut. Maybe I'm imagining things.

Anne parks the bike at the edge of the trail and cuts the engine. We slide off in unison, remove our helmets. Leafless trees give way to a golden path peppered with orange and red. Small animal tracks imprint the surrounding dirt. An abandoned tunnel marks the end of this trail. My friends and I used to hang there to party—until Rick's brother got drunk and almost died playing chicken with the trains. Been a while since any of us has been back.

Anne slips behind a cluster of bushes and emerges with a backpack. There's a sleeping bag rolled up and tied to the bottom.

"You've been planning this for a while," I say. It's meant to sound teasing, but my voice chokes with surprise. I'm supposed to be the romantic.

Anne slings the pack over her shoulders and extends a hand. "A little premeditated romance of my own."

Her bag clinks while we walk along the path in silence, our fingers interlaced. The air is thick with the scent of rotting leaves and damp earth. "It's a perfect night," I say.

Anne smiles. "And we're just getting started."

Her voice is a soft purr of seduction and something darker, some kind of cryptic warning. But as we round the corner and the rusted tunnel looms into view, I ignore the feeling and my focus shifts. Even under the faded light of the stars, the graffiti-covered walls take me back to another—less complicated—time.

Anne drops the bag on the ground and fishes inside for a camping lantern. She flicks the switch and the inside of the tunnel lights up. Random weeds snake through the soil. Faded candy wrappers and rusted beer cans sprinkle the ground. Someone has kicked away the bricks that once lined a fire pit at its base, but it's evident no one has been here since the trains stopped running.

"Gather wood," Anne says. "I brought paper and matches. I'll fix the fire pit."

I'm about to protest and suggest the smoke will attract attention, but Anne is already clearing a space and laying out the sleeping bag, focused on her mission.

I load my arms with loose branches and pieces of old wood, while she sits cross-legged on the sleeping bag, crumpling paper into fist-size balls. Together we stack the smaller sticks, and then the branches until we've made a wooden teepee. She lights a match.

The paper curls and smolders, ignites the first flame, begins devouring the wood. The fire crackles and hisses. A silver thread of smoke spirals into the sky. The match burns down to her fingertips and she shakes it until the flame extinguishes.

I stretch out and motion for Anne to come closer. She rummages through her pack instead, withdrawing a bottle of vodka. When our eyes meet, there's a light in hers I don't quite understand. "I hope this is all right," she says. "Thomas's stash is a bit low. It was either this or tequila. And I hate tequila."

I hesitate for a split second, worried—confused—about why she's acting so strange. But then she nibbles on her lower lip, and all rational thoughts disappear.

I snatch the bottle from her and twist off the cap. The alcohol burns my throat as I drink. Another long pull and intoxicating warmth spreads throughout my body. "Impressive prep skills," I say, and wipe my mouth. Hand back the bottle. "You must have been a Girl Scout."

Anne snuggles into me, the booze tucked between her legs. Her fingers trail along my inner thigh. "Nah. They kicked me out of that club," she says.

"So how long do you think before the cavalry shows up?" I say, only half in jest. I'm fast becoming intoxicated by Anne's touch.

Her finger circles my knee cap. "I'm afraid it's just the two of us."

Goose bumps ripple along my skin. There's an underlying sexiness to her words that leave me ragged and shallow. She's so hot I forget about going slow.

I shift so that we're facing each other and burrow my hand in her hair, hold the base of her neck. She slides her hands under my shirt and eases it up over my head. Rakes her fingernails down the front of my chest. I grip her hips, cup her ass, and flip her so she's on top. Her breath fans over me.

I lean forward and reclaim her lips, desperate to kiss every inch of her mouth. Need presses against my chest, crushing and hard.

Anne's shirt rides up and my fingers explore the satin skin of her belly. When I skim the waistband of her jeans, she gasps.

I look up and her eyes shine.

"Anne, I—"

Her lips cram against mine. Desperate. Hungry. Desire surges through my body like wildfire. I scrape my teeth along her lower lip, drawing out a whimper.

Anne tugs off her shirt and throws it aside. A red lace bra stares back at me. Nothing else. And the swell of her breasts against that lace is driving me mad. "You're so beautiful," I say.

Our hands are everywhere. She is soft and hungry, breathless and frantic. Her fingers expertly navigate my body, kneading the tight muscles on my shoulders, my back. Then our kisses grow slower, filled with promise and passion. I am so lost in the moment that when she jerks away, my first instinct is pain.

"The fire," she says, and points to the waning flame.

I add another log, poke at the smoldering ashes with a long stick. When it reignites, I turn back to find Anne on her knees, the bottle of vodka on her lips, her bra cast aside. I swallow hard, my eyes locked on her naked chest. She tilts her head back and drinks. Liquid drips from her mouth and down her neck, dribbles onto her flesh.

"Holy shit," I say.

I grab the bottle and suck back a swig. My head spins. Anne drags me toward her and the bottle slips from my hand and spills onto the blanket. My mind is fuzzy, hazy with lust as I greedily lick the alcohol from her skin.

Her dark hair fans out on the sleeping bag like raven feathers. She is bare from the waist up, the tiny bumps on her flesh raised from the cold or maybe my touch. "You're perfect," I say.

She flattens her palms against the top of my head and pushes my mouth lower. My tongue drags across her flesh. She tastes like cinnamon.

"Tell me you want me," she whispers.

I growl in response. Tug at the waistband of her jeans. The button pops loose.

Anne squirms under me. "Say it," she says.

The words catch in my throat as I paw at her skin, as some animalistic need pulses through me. I ease her jeans off her hips, down over her pale thighs. Slide them all the way off. She's naked but for a pair of sexy red lace panties.

"Henry," she says as I'm removing her underwear, my jeans and my briefs. She inhales sharply, and for a second, neither of us moves. "Henry," she whispers. "Tell me I'm all you'll ever need."

I roll my body over hers in response, and her legs tangle with mine. We become lost in kisses, in warm skin and touches. I tease her with my teeth, nipping and sucking, pushing my knee between her legs to separate them. And then we're moving together, breathing together, our bodies in perfect rhythm. Her thighs press against my hips, pulling me closer. We quicken the pace. My heart thumps so fast it almost implodes.

Right when I'm about to lose control, Anne calls out my name, and then it hits me like a shock of white heat, a trembling sensation that rips through my core.

I pull her close and tuck her trembling body against mine. Unable to speak, I kiss her forehead, the corner of her mouth. Her lips curl. I give in to the moment and close my eyes. The ground spins beneath me.

I am in love with Anne.

She is not seducing me. I am not seducing her. We are choosing to be together.

"I love you," she says, a soft whisper in the night.

My response is a contented sigh. There's so much feeling wrapped up inside me right now—too much. Love feels inadequate. This is so much more.

"Henry," she says, before I can find the right response, to tell her I love her too. A pause and then with more urgency, "Henry!" I'm ripped out of my trance. She scrambles out of my arms, eyes wide and frightened, finger pointing at the fire. I sit upright.

The edge of the sleeping bag is burning. I glance at the

open alcohol bottle and jump to my feet, kicking aside the vodka and folding the sleeping bag in half and in half again, smothering the blaze. I must look ridiculous.

The whole situation is ridiculous.

Anne begins to laugh.

Quiet at first, then until we're both in hysterics, struck by the absurdity of it all. Standing together naked, not quite drunk from the alcohol and fueled by reckless abandon.

"Talk about a buzz kill," Anne says with a snort. She stoops to pick up her underwear, T-shirt, and the vodka, holds the bottle up to the moonlight. "There's barely any booze left."

She takes a swig and hands it to me. As I swallow what's left, she puts on her clothes and reaches into her bag, pulls out a couple of spray-paint cans—one black, one red. When I've finished getting myself dressed, she hands one to me. With the black, she draws a giant letter *H* on an inner tunnel wall. I move in quick with a red plus sign and she follows with an *A*. I draw a heart and she moves on to another clean part of the tunnel.

"Anne, what are we doing?"

"Letting loose," she says. And then with far less humor, "Life should be fun. We can never lose that, Henry. No matter what happens to us. No matter what anyone says."

I swallow. Nod. Try to read between the lines. But before I can analyze, she shakes the can.

We alternate painting with kissing, plastering the tunnel with our initials and hearts, covering past artwork. I count more than twenty *Hs* and *As* before our spray cans are empty and we're exhausted.

For a minute, we stand together, admiring our work.

My cell buzzes, breaking the mood. I know without looking it's my mother. I don't take out my phone but Anne knows it too. My body tenses. There's no place I'd rather be.

"We should go," Anne says, and rests her head against my shoulder. The scent of alcohol whispers from her lips. "It's late and soon your mother *will* send out the cavalry."

She's right, but I'm nervous. I'm far from drunk. Is she? "Maybe we should sober up first."

Anne looks at me and scoffs. Touches her finger to her nose. "I'm not even buzzed, Henry." As though to further prove her point, she shrugs out of my embrace and bends down to gather our supplies. The sleeping bag is charred and reeks of smoke, but she unfolds it and rolls it back up anyway, her movements mechanical and practiced.

I snuff out the fire, disoriented by the abrupt change in her attitude. I know something's still not right.

She heaves the pack over her shoulders and holds out her hand.

"We should talk," I say.

"I'm fine," she says. I want to believe her, but her voice slurs just a little.

As we make our way back, I pay close attention to the way she walks and talks, lingering where possible for extended kisses. Halfway to the road, I carve our initials into a tree trunk, taking the time to make the cuts extra deep. By the time we reach her bike, I've run out of stall tactics.

Once we're seated, the bike jolts forward. Anne's body is rigid, straight, and tense. She twists the throttle and we hit the gravel. My heart thumps with something akin to fear.

Anne expertly maneuvers Clarice along the rustic trail and my stomach settles. She's pissed, not drunk. And even though I'm annoyed she won't tell me what's wrong, relief winds through me.

Anne picks up speed. The scenery blurs, blends into one continuous line of forest. We move so fast I don't even see the car coming toward us.

"Watch out," I yell.

But it's like she can't hear me. She takes a sharp left corner and ducks into an alley. I spare a glance back and the car careens out of sight. My pulse throbs, my head screams. I know this is stupid, but with every near miss, it's like I'm mainlining adrenaline. I don't want it to stop.

I let out a yelp and turn back just as Anne swerves to miss a pothole. Clarice wobbles and jerks to the right. The front tire turns sharply. Anne tries to hold on, but it's too late. The tires slide out from underneath the bike.

My body shoots upward and when Clarice hits the

ground, I'm thrown loose. Everything blurs. The asphalt bites and burns my skin. I smell the coppery taint of blood.

There's the squeal of metal.

The crash of breaking glass.

My voice cracks, screaming for Anne.

And then—

CHAPTER TWENTY-FOUR
Anne

My vision floods with blinding white light.

A blade of pain slices through my skull, so sharp it sends my head slamming back against the hard, unyielding mattress. I'm cold, disoriented. Terrified.

The scent of clean tingles my nostrils and singes my skin. A series of *beep, beep, beeps* echoes like a heartbeat. I close my eyes, willing myself to return to the dark dreamy unconscious where everything seemed clear and peaceful.

My mother's voice breaks the trance.

"Anne?"

My eyelashes flutter as I try to emerge from the fog. I open my eyes and her face blurs into view. Pale. Worried. The deep shadows under her eyes make her look older. I blink twice but she doesn't disappear. "Where am I?" I say, my throat hoarse.

She rests her head on my chest.

"You had us so scared," she says, choking. "You've been in and out for hours, almost unconscious for two days. We thought you might slip into a coma." A tear slides over her cheek. "The doctor says you're going to be okay, though. You were very lucky, ladybug."

I shift and a sharp pain radiates up my left leg. "Everything hurts."

My mother lifts her head, reaches for my hand, and squeezes so tight I flinch. I bite my lip to stop from calling out.

"There was an accident," she says. "Your motorcycle . . ."

"Clarice?"

"I'm afraid it's in rough shape." She's never liked Clarice, the fact that I ride, but this isn't an *I-told-you-so* moment. Her eyes cloud with sympathy and I'm overwhelmed with the unnerving sense that she's not telling me something, that there's so much more I don't know, have forgotten. "Thomas already has it in the shop."

She rubs her cool hand along my forearm. "Do you remember anything about the accident?"

I close my eyes and think, think, think. No matter how hard I search the dark alcove of my mind, I come up blank. It's like my brain is filled with black air, a thick blob against whatever lurks behind it.

"You'd been drinking a little," my mother says. The image of a vodka bottle flashes across my mind. I'm laughing, tipping my head back as liquid dribbles from the side of my mouth, down my chin, onto my chest. The background is fuzzy and out of focus.

"I can only assume that's why you let Henry drive."

Henry?

Holy shit, Henry. The memories begin to rewind in slow motion. His hands wrapped tight around my waist, our movements in perfect unison. The bike shifts, we begin to fall. I can't hold on, can't regain control.

My mother's words play back. Stop. Repeat. *I can only assume that's why you let Henry drive.*

But he wasn't, I want to say, the confession stuck like molasses in my throat.

"At least you were both smart about that. I know how protective you are of your motorcycle," she says. "But he wasn't used to driving it and—"

My blood turns to ice, my skin cools. I can almost *feel* the color drain from my face as more pieces of the accident begin locking into place. The tunnel, the booze, the sleeping bag catching fire, Henry's kiss, his hands all over me, our bodies intertwined—

Henry.

I try to sit upright and a sharp pain shoots along my rib cage. "Is he . . . ?"

"He's fine." My mother eases my shoulders back onto the pillow. Despite her efforts, I'm not buying it. Something's off. "He has a few cuts and scrapes, and they kept him overnight. Nothing a little rest won't fix. You're both very lucky." She drops her voice to a harsh whisper. "But what were you *thinking*?"

I barely hear her question amid the chaos swirling in my brain. The echo of a police siren hums in my subconscious. Ambulance lights flash and blink, blink and flash. My stomach rolls as I recall swerving Clarice through the narrow streets, driving too fast, way, way too fast. The screech of metal reverberates in my mind. And then—

Henry's terrified cry rips through my vision.

"No, no, no . . ."

Wet tears well at the corner of my eyes and I squeeze them shut. But streaks of grief roll down my face, pool under my chin. My mother is lying—it's the only thing that makes sense. Because if he's really all right, not broken, just bruised, then why doesn't she know Henry wasn't driving?

She reaches for my hand. "Ladybug, don't cry. Henry is going to be just fine. I promise. Everything is going to be okay. You could have gotten yourself in real trouble."

Something sticky blooms in my stomach and then I get it. Why nothing makes sense. Henry has lied to my mother, to the police, to *everyone*. Sacrificed himself—his family's name—to keep me safe.

I force myself to remember, to slip back into a dreamlike state. I'm sprawled on the ground. The asphalt around me

glitters with broken glass. In the background, the rising drone
of a siren pulses behind my temples.

Henry's face emerges from the haze, scratched and cut,
features pinched.

"Jesus, Anne, what the hell was that?"

*A trickle of blood runs down the side of his cheek. I reach up,
but he bats away my hand.*

"We don't have much time." His voice is angry, cruel, desperate. *My heart cracks a little from the pain.* "I was driving,
Anne. Do you hear me?" *He runs his hand through his hair.*
"Fuck." Henry leans in close, almost presses his bloodied face
up against mine. *"Listen to me: If they find out you were driving, you're done."*

I blink open my eyes. The tears come back and my voice
wobbles. "But . . ."

My mother silences me with a finger to my lips and I'm
struck by another moment of truth. She *knows* what Henry's
done. That I was reckless and stupid. That if the police knew
I was driving, I'd be in jail, not the hospital.

I want to scream that it's her fault. That because of the
hurtful words she said to me, the fresh wounds she carved, I
spun out of control. I put Henry, put *us*, in danger.

"I need to see Henry," I say. "Is he in the waiting room?" The
slight tremor in my voice gives me away and my mother looks
beyond me, out through the window. Rain streaks the glass and
in the distance a dark cloud hovers over the thick forest.

"Mom? Where is Henry?"

"He's at home, baby," she says. "Please get some rest. We can talk about Henry later."

Fresh panic pricks at my skin. Why isn't he here? I scan the window ledge, the side table, even the floor, but there are no flowers, no balloons, no cards of sympathy.

Isn't he worried?

Doesn't he care?

I try again to sit upright, but my mother pushes me back down with a steady hand. "Anne, please. It's important you get some sleep. You have a concussion. I'm sure Henry will be here to see you when you're feeling better."

My mouth goes dry. "He hasn't been here at all?"

She shakes her head and tries for an expression of encouragement, but I've long ago cracked her emotional code. I've been unconscious for two days and Henry hasn't visited my room once.

Neither of us thinks this is okay.

A knock at the door halts fresh tears, but my hope evaporates when Sam enters. As much as I like her, she's not Henry. She carries a bouquet of daisies and a sheepish smile, says hello to my mom.

"I know this is super cliché," she says, setting the vase on the night table next to me. "I couldn't figure out anything else." She flops down on a chair. "You had me worried."

Despite my inner turmoil I'm touched that she's here.

"Sam, this is—"

"Oh, we've met," my mother cuts in, "Your friend has been here a couple of times."

"You were like, totally out of it," Sam says, with a chuckle that morphs into a sigh. "Want to talk?"

My mother stands and smooths her skirt with the palm of her hands, leaving sweaty prints on the suede. "I think I'll go find you something to eat," she says nervously, like she's not sure what I'll say to Sam. "There must be something better than this hospital food, right?"

She slips out the door without glancing back and my body starts to shake.

"You scared her pretty good," Sam says, and reaches into her purse for a chocolate bar and her phone. She sets both on the nightstand and I cling to hope by a thin thread. If I can just *talk* to Henry, we'll figure all of this out. . . .

An ominous shadow covers the hole in my chest. Maybe Henry isn't here because he's angry, upset at the terrible, awful position I've put him in. Pissed off at having to cover for my recklessness and stupidity.

"Sam, I need a favor," I say. I'm a quivering mess. "My mother took my phone and I really want to talk to Henry."

She looks at me sideways. "I get it. You guys have to get your stories straight."

I know it's a test, but I won't take the bait. Whatever rumors she believes will have to be enough for now.

"I can't—"

Sam waves off my response and punches a number into her cell. The phone unlocks and Henry's contact information swims onto the screen.

"You've got ten minutes," she says, standing. At the door, she pauses. "I'll be outside if you need me."

I nod. "Thank you," I whisper, but she's already out the door, and a hollow ringtone starts echoing in my ear.

On the third ring, someone picks up and my stomach clenches at the unexpected sound of a stern feminine voice. "Mrs. Tudor? It's Anne. Anne Boleyn."

There's a moment of silence punctuated by the *thump-gallop-thump* of my heart. Maybe she didn't hear me or there's a bad connection on the line or—

"What can I do for you, Ms. Boleyn?" The tone of her voice is colder than fresh snow.

"Is Henry there?"

"He's resting, finally," she snaps. "I suppose he has you to thank for this mess."

It's not a question, so I don't bother with a response. Instead, I say, "Will you let him know I called?"

My gaze flits to the clock on the wall. I wonder how long before my mother charges through the door with real food and a false smile.

Henry's mother clucks her tongue and sighs, though it sounds as if she's breathing out of her nose like some kind of nightmarish dragon. I shudder. "No, I don't think I will, Anne."

Confusion muddles my response. "Don't think you'll—"

"Let him know that you called," she says. "Actually, I think it's best you stay away from my son."

I open my mouth to defend myself but no sound comes out.

"Henry won't tell me the whole story about what happened," she says. "However, I do know this: He's lying. I don't believe Henry was driving your motorcycle. Not for one second. He's obviously covering for you."

Guilt renders me speechless. She's right and there's nothing I can do about it, not one damn—

"Henry would never have lied to me before," she continues. "But since you've gotten your claws into him, I don't know what to think anymore. I see what you're doing, young lady. Flaunting yourself. It's disgusting."

The clock moves forward another minute as though in slow motion. Tick

tock.

The numbers blur under the haze of my tears. I want to hang up, to start over, to wind back the time by hand and forget the hospital, the accident, the tunnel—

No, not the tunnel.

I flash back to the moment Henry's hands start caressing my skin. Lips exploring my flesh. I swallow, fighting the sweet, dangerous memory, and shut my eyes briefly against the rising wave of longing.

"It's not like that," I say.

"You may have seduced Henry, Ms. Boleyn, but you have *not* fooled me. I won't have him dragged into some kind of scandal. Stay away from him."

I swallow my nerves and clear my throat. "You don't know what you're asking, Mrs. Tudor. I love—"

A merciless chuckle crackles through the line. "Love? Please. Henry doesn't have time for these pathetic high school games. He is destined for greatness, Ms. Boleyn. And I won't allow some tramp to get in the way of that."

My hand grips the phone so tight I'm sure my veins will explode. "You know nothing about me."

"I know enough," she says. "Keep your dirty hands off of him. I won't ask again."

There's a charged beat between us, a terrifying moment where decisions happen. Stay on the line and fight, or give in.

"I mean it," she says with a sigh so deep I know I'm already done for. "If you care for Henry at all, let him go. You don't belong in his world."

CHAPTER TWENTY-FIVE
Henry

I hover at Anne's locker, like I'm waiting to walk her to class, hold her hand, pretend everything's normal. Stupid, since I know she's not coming—and nothing's been normal since the accident. Now that I know she'll be okay, worry has morphed into anger. I'm pissed off that I'm paying for her mistakes.

While she's at home healing, trying to move on, I'm avoiding questions, making excuses, dodging those *I-told-you-so* stares. Does she even know the shit storm she's caused?

My version of the accident has earned me a week of my mother's house arrest. Stripped of my electronics and the keys to my car, and issued a chauffeur to ensure I don't go out of bounds. I'm dropped off at school and picked up like a damn kindergartener.

I guess it's better than the alternative. The combination of my mother's smooth talking and our family name has kept me out of jail.

And yet, no matter how furious I am, I can't get Anne off my mind. She has this way of getting into your blood and now I'm so scared to lose the high, I'll do anything— whatever it takes—to hold on.

I slam my fist against the wall and curse.

"Temper, temper," clucks a voice in my periphery. "Dude, you have to keep that shit in check."

I give John the finger without even turning around. I'd recognize that cockiness blindfolded and drunk. My response is met with a chuckle.

"Sounds like you need to get a lot of things under control," pipes in another voice.

I spin around to scowl at Catherine, and I'm momentarily and unexpectedly frozen. We haven't been this close in days, weeks. Her presence unnerves me and puts me at ease all at once.

Things with Catherine were simple by comparison. She's predictable. Tudor-approved. Anne is . . . not.

"Something on your mind?" I say.

Catherine folds her arms across her chest and shifts her hips to one side. Her hair is blonder than I remember and she's wearing her makeup differently—dark, bold, *not her.* On the surface, she pulls it off, the sense that she's over it, over us, and moved on. But I see past that thick eyeliner to the truth.

Despite everything, there's something comforting about knowing she still cares, no matter how superficially.

Because Anne is foreign and unknown, often disconcerting. Maddening. She throws me off my game and makes me question—me. My future. But even though I'm pissed, I don't regret standing up for her, shouldering the fault. I got off with a warning about driving too fast and without a proper motorcycle license. The cops didn't bother testing me for alcohol, barely questioned my story. One of the many perks that come from being a Tudor, I guess. Anne would have been burned at the stake.

"Give me your phone," I say to John. The morning bell rings and the halls begin to empty as students file into class, gossiping and groaning about homework and Mondays and how many weeks and days are left until Christmas break. Some wave, others pretend they're not looking, but no one stops. It's as though they're giving us a wide berth for whatever comes next. I hold out my hand. "It's a simple request, man."

John clears his throat, averts his gaze. "I can't let you call her."

My jaw leaps. "Why the fuck would you care?"

"Whoa. Chill," John says, and holds up his hands in self defense, like I might hit him if he says the wrong thing.

I take a step back and lean against Anne's locker.

"Your mother gave us strict instructions," John says. "She's . . . convincing."

"You're shitting me, right?" My eyes go so wide I'll bet I look alien. "Since when do you listen to what she says?"

"Since when do you swear so much?" Catherine snaps.

I know what she's getting at, but I refuse the bait. "Fuck this," I say, and try to push past her. "And fuck both of you."

Catherine's expression registers shock and I recoil.

Jesus. What the hell is wrong with me?

Her cool fingers wrap around my wrist, holding me in place. "We're worried about you, Henry," she says, her voice soft and tender. She searches my face, expecting some kind of reaction, maybe looking for a sign I've heard or even care what she has to say. "The accident . . ."

"I'm fine," I say through gritted teeth. My fists clench, but Catherine doesn't let go.

"Still, man, you took a serious risk." John runs a hand through his disheveled hair. "I mean, what were you doing? You can't learn to drive a motorcycle in one night."

"He didn't," Catherine says, and drops my wrist. My arm falls limp. Gone is the glimmer of compassion, the false sympathy. Her expression hardens. "He's covering for *her*. It's the only thing that makes sense."

My limbs feel like lead. She's not the first to suggest this—the police, my mother.

"Is that true?"

I shift my gaze, focus on the window in the classroom across the hall. The teacher writes something on the whiteboard and I squint to read it. The swirl of letters doesn't make sense, some kind of poem, maybe. I've just about made out the first sentence when a shadow moves in front of the glass and blocks my view.

"That chick's not worth it," John says. "She's trash."

It happens fast. I grab his jacket, spin him around, and slam him against Anne's locker. Draw back a fist. "Say that again," I growl.

His face pales, but he doesn't let up. He's not the type. My hand presses against his throat, tight enough so there's a semicircle of white skin encircling my fingertips.

"Henry, what's gotten into you?" Catherine says, tugging at my biceps. "Stop this. Stop it now. Why are you throwing everything away for her?"

I am precariously close to punching my best friend in the face, but I'm aware of the small crowd gathering behind us, the hushed whispers. A school fight would be a direct violation not only of council rules, but also Medina Academy's Code of Conduct. I can't take expulsion on top of house arrest.

I loosen the grip around John's neck. Drop my hands.

He adjusts his shirt, his jacket, rubs at the red line across his throat. "Keep on moving, people," he says, addressing the students milling around us like paparazzi, anxious for even one nugget of gossip. He flashes one of those signature crazy-ass grins. "Henry's boning up on his tackling moves. He's out of practice."

As the last of the stragglers disappear into a classroom,

Catherine steps between us, using her body as a shield. I thrust myself against a locker to avoid her touch and bash my elbow.

"Are we done with this crap?" she says, glancing at me, then John, then back at me. She presses her lips together as though deep in thought. "Look Henry, she's not who you think she is."

"Right, like I should trust you."

No matter how confused and angry I am, I know Anne doesn't deserve this shit.

A nervous glance passes between Catherine and John. Catherine opens her mouth, but John holds up his hand, pretending to be chivalrous, like he should be the one to deliver the news.

"Word is, she gets around," he says.

Anger fills me. "I'd expect this kind of bullshit from her," I say, jerking my thumb at Catherine. "But bowing down to gossip? That's not your style, John."

"Just listen," Catherine says. "What do you know about her? The person she was before she came to Medina?"

I try to ignore the questions, but Catherine's touched on a nerve. Anne's confession has been on my mind the past couple of days, and I'm ashamed to admit, I've been looking for gaps in her story. Something she left out. It's not that I don't believe her. . . . Fuck. Maybe I do have a tinge of doubt.

I shake my head and scowl. Anne didn't lie—not about

that. And questioning her, when she's not here to defend herself, makes me no better than her sister's asshole boyfriend.

"I've had enough," I say. "I gotta get to class."

I start walking but John blocks my path. Looks me dead straight in the eyes. "I know you're too wrapped up in her to see it, but she's a straight-up whore, man."

Fire erupts in my chest and I clamp my teeth together to stop from roaring. My tone is low and menacing, dangerous and slow. "Shut. The hell. Up."

John takes a step back. It's enough to avoid a punch, but I'm not opposed to lunging forward and dropping him to the ground. Consequences be damned, this time I won't stop. "You don't want to push me," I say.

The *click-clack* of heels echoes down the hallway and the vice principal emerges in the distance, taps her wrist. Her voice sing-songs its ways to us. "You're late, my pets."

She keeps walking, but the interruption is enough for me to catch my bearings.

"We've been friends a long time, bro," John says, calmer now. "You know I want what's best for you. Maybe this wasn't the right way."

"You're still pissed because she burned you off. Get over it, *bro*." My voice lowers to a growl. "Unless you can't." A lightbulb goes off in my head. "That's it, isn't it? You've got a thing for her."

John averts his gaze. "No, but I think she's got something for me."

"Keep dreaming, asshole," I spit out. "She's way out of your league."

John lifts his chin. "Think what you want, but the things she says to me. Shit, man, it's harsh." He makes a face of disgust, curls his lip. "She's always rubbing up against me, talking about sex. We have chemistry together."

My expression changes and John holds up his hands again. "Class, man. We have chemistry *class* together."

"I've seen it too," Catherine says. "She's got eyes on him. And others. You can deny it all you want, Henry, but you're covering up her mistakes while she's stringing you along like a puppy. Sooner or later, she'll betray you."

A knot forms in my chest. "You're both off base," I say, but some of the conviction is gone. I can't help but think about what went down with Anne's sister, and it makes me feel like shit. Because as much as I want to believe her, there's a sliver of doubt. "She's confident. That doesn't make her a whore."

Catherine tucks a strand of hair behind her ear. "There's a difference between innocent teasing and—"

"I'm not buying it," I say, louder now.

"We just want you to be careful," John says. "You've known her, what? A couple of months? You've already thrown yourself on your sword for her. Is she worth it? You could've gotten a DUI, man. You think guys with DUIs win elections?"

Another piece of my resolve crumbles. It's so easy to believe John's jealous, or just following Catherine's lead—he's always had a crush on her. My best friend's no angel, but this confrontation goes against everything I know about him.

He steps closer. "Come on, Henry. You see it, right? You're ditching events, lying to your mom, to your friends." He pats his chest. "To me." I open my mouth to say something, but John doesn't stop. "You show up for practice, but you're not even there. She's, like, bewitched you."

Confusion blurs my focus. I scour memories of the past few weeks, the last couple of days, searching for clues that they're right, some indication that I've been blind to a giant neon-red flag. But even Anne's confession about Mary isn't enough for me to give up on her. Deep down I want to believe her. I have to. Because without trust, what's left?

"Give us a chance to show you," Catherine says. "We're not asking you to break up with her. Just let us prove to you that she isn't right for you. When you've seen the evidence . . ."

"There won't be any, because she's not who you think," I say. But a sliver of doubt has sliced through my shield and is worming its way into my confidence. I push it back. "You won't find anything."

"Maybe that's true," John says, and tilts his head. "If so, I'll be first in line to apologize."

"Me too," Catherine says.

"Fine," I say, voice tight. "But when you come back with nothing, that's the end of it. Right? You'll give it a rest and accept her?"

"Deal," John says. "We'll all welcome her with open arms."

Catherine nods, and for the moment, I trust them, hoping they truly want what's best for me. And yet as I watch their retreating forms, I can't figure out why the weight around my heart refuses to lift.

CHAPTER TWENTY-SIX
Anne

My stomach is twisted, all tied up in knots, wondering if I'll see Henry, scared that I won't. It's been a week since everything went from so right to so horribly wrong.

I'm convinced he won't be there, that he's already given up on me, when I spot him. He's leaning up against my locker, looking helpless and hopeless, as messed up as me.

I start walking faster and almost crash into his chest.

"Anne," Henry says so soft it's almost a whisper. His hand winds into my hair and pulls me close. I'm breathless and weightless, desperate and raw. His lips graze my mouth, and my body turns to liquid.

"You never came to see me," I say, when he pulls away. I've spent hours staring at the ceiling, waiting and crying, dreaming of going back to that moment, when everything was—

Perfect.

Henry nuzzles his chin into my hair, kisses the top of my head. "I wanted to," he says. "At first I was furious—what we did, Anne . . ."

"Was stupid," I say.

He nods as though waiting for me to say more, to explain why I acted so out of control. I try to shut out the guilt. I'm not ready to tell him what my mother said, how she thinks I'm to blame for Mary. A part of me is scared Henry thinks so too.

"I've been grounded all week," Henry says, and runs his hand though his hair. "Shit. That makes it sound like she took away my teddy bear or something."

I know without him saying, he's lost a lot more. "You shouldn't have taken the fall for me," I say. "I'm not worth—"

Henry silences me with a kiss. It's tender and potent, erasing some of the fear and the doubt.

"I did what I needed to do for you, for us, " he says, drawing me into his arms. "This will blow over." He pulls back a little, looks into my eyes. "But it can't happen again." His tone is stern. "I can't afford another mistake." He wraps his arms around me. Holds on so tight I could burst. "Jesus, I've missed you."

I nod, because there are no words here that work, and wipe away the tears with the back of my hand.

"How long until your mom cuts you loose?" I finally say.

"Tonight—if I'm good," he says. At my raised eyebrow, he shrugs. "I'm having dinner with a Harvard guy. To make up for missing—"

"The event you skipped when we were at the theater," I say. I flash back to our first kiss and my jaw hurts from smiling so wide.

Henry kisses the tip of my nose. "I'd do it again." He waggles his eyebrows. "And again."

Henry opens my locker, peering inside with a sheepish grin. He pulls out a bouquet of wilted flowers. "I wasn't sure when you'd be back," he says. "I picked these a few days ago."

"From the courtyard?" I say with a smirk.

He shrugs. "Best I could do with my limited resources."

"They're perfect." I kiss his blushing cheek. "You're perfect."

The bell chimes and Henry presses a mass of paper into my hand. "I wrote a letter for every day we couldn't talk," he says. "Toward the end they get a bit cheesy."

By the time I hit class, I've read them all through. He's right. Some are cheesy. But I don't care. I've soaked in every word. Through them, my understanding of his feelings—the worry, confusion, frustration, even anger—deepens.

Now, as the class erupts in the chaos of prelunch socialization, a silhouette falls across my desk. I know without looking it's Marie—her presence is an ominous cloud, a shadow of foreboding. I've heard more of the rumors and know she's one of the girls behind them.

I stare at my open textbook, doodle in the margins. When I stop, the pen bleeds ink onto the page.

Finally, I look up. Marie is flanked by two henchwomen, Liz and some girl I've never met.

"Anne, darling, we'd love to chat," she says.

"Thanks, I'll pass," I say, gathering my textbooks. My hip catches on the edge of the desk as I stand, too rushed to get away. Pain spiderwebs across my midsection. The doctors have stopped worrying about my head, but the rest of my body has yet to fully heal.

"I think you'll change your mind," Marie says. She takes a step closer, so close I can see the outline of her bra through her thin white blouse. "Do you know what people are saying about you?"

"Because I care?" I swallow the little white lie, stuff it down so far it disappears in the pit of my stomach. The classroom is empty now and it's just the four of us in the room.

"Bet you'd care if Henry knew," Marie says.

I pull my books into my chest. "Henry doesn't listen to gossip."

"Maybe not now," she says. "But the rumors will just poke and poke." She thrusts her finger at me and almost touches my arm, punctuating her point. "Everything you do will be under close scrutiny. You won't be able to cough without someone telling Henry you've caught mono."

"The once innocent gossip will transform into lies," Liz chimes in.

Marie perches on the edge of my desk. "And the lies just keep growing and growing until—"

"Henry snaps," the nameless girl says, ending the sentence with a cluck of her tongue.

"He's not like that," I say, though my voice trembles a little, betraying my doubt.

Guilt creeps under my skin. It's because of me his life has become stressful. With Catherine, he had acceptance, approval, solid footing. I've brought him nothing but trouble.

"It's not too late," Marie says. She reaches out toward me and rests her hand on my forearm. I resist the urge to flinch, to pull away. "There's still time for you to change what people are saying about you."

I choke on impossibility. "How?"

Liz shrugs her shoulders. "By hanging out with us, for starters," she says. "Instead of avoiding us, join the group."

I scan her features, looking deep into the corners of her eyes for the mockery I'm sure is there. Do they think I'm an idiot? That I'm stupid enough to believe they want to spend time with me—the school misfit, the girl who knocked Queen Catherine—their friend—off her throne?

"Funny," I say, and bend down to pick up my purse. Henry's letters poke out and I stuff them down, afraid they'll fall out and that Marie and her friends will see them. "I get it," I say, feigning nonchalance. "You don't like me, and that's okay. I've never been in with the mean girls. All that really matters is what Henry thinks."

Marie's mouth twitches. "Yeah, we figured you'd say that," she says. "Because Henry said the same thing."

My eyes widen. "He did?"

Liz nods. "Of course. He really cares for you."

"More than we thought," Marie adds. "We didn't want to believe it, because we just assumed Henry and Catherine would always be together, you know?" She twirls a piece of her hair around a well-manicured fingertip—bright red with black polka dots—and shrugs. "Henry set us straight."

They stare at me expectantly, like they're waiting for me to have that moment of clarity, to thrust my hand up and shout, "Aha!" Instead, I regard them with caution, try to figure out their angle.

"So, you think we should, what? Eat lunch together? Maybe get pedicures?" The words snap from my lips with the razor-sharp edge of disbelief. "We could even start dressing alike."

She giggles. "You're cute," she says. "But we had something else in mind."

Liz slips her hand into the pocket of her blouse and withdraws a slip of paper. "This is my address. I'm having a party tonight. You should come."

"Henry will be there after he attends some function, one

last demonstration of his renewed commitment to his future," Marie adds, rolling her eyes.

I bite my lip. It's true Henry won't be grounded anymore, but that doesn't mean we're free to go out. At least not alone. I haven't decided how to deal with his mother's warning to stay away from her son, don't know whether or not I should even tell Henry. This party may be the only chance we have to talk.

"Why the hesitation?" Marie says. "You know you want to come."

"Will Catherine be there?" I hate myself for asking, but I'm not strong enough for that fight yet.

Marie and Liz exchange glances. "Yes," Liz says. "Look. She's been through a lot, between Arthur and . . . this. She gets it, though. Henry's moved on. We've been friends a long time, and change is hard."

I stare down at the ground, count the black scuffmarks on the tile.

Something stirs in my stomach, a sharp little thrill. Maybe I'm making a mistake and this is one big joke. It's likely I'll show up and no one will be there, or worse, they all will and I'll be the center of attention again, the butt of their collective joke.

But with Henry in my corner now, I'm stronger.

When I look up, Marie and her friends are staring at me like they're made of stone. Expressions unreadable. Cold masks that betray nothing, offer no comfort.

"Well?" Marie says, and the firm set of her mouth cracks into a smile. "You coming, or what?"

I inhale a deep breath. Blow it out as I throw my purse over my shoulder and shrug, faking an indifference I don't feel. I may be about to make the biggest mistake of my life, but Marie's right. Henry is hanging on by a loose thread, and I have to do something to ease the tension. He's sacrificed so much for me—surely I can handle a few hours with his life-long friends. "Sure," I say. "Why the hell not?"

CHAPTER TWENTY-SEVEN

Henry

The open notebook glares at me. Sentences I've scrawled across the paper in black ink—an effort to unjumble my thoughts, figure out the lies.

This is for your own good.

You're just like your brother.

Your father would be proud.

All the untruths my family, friends, perfect strangers have tried to make me believe.

But my father *wouldn't* be proud.

I'm *nothing* like Arthur.

And no matter what argument anyone produces, whatever evidence my friends think they'll find, keeping me from Anne is most definitely *not* for my own good.

I slam the notebook shut. I'm so angry I'm beyond language, beyond rational thought. All I see when I close my eyes are my mother's lips, going back on her word, grounding me for just "one more night."

What the hell kind of game is she playing?

I loosen my tie, glance at my cell. It's a useless piece of crap. My mother may have given it back to me, but not before deleting Anne's contact information. I tried texting, but the message came back blocked, undeliverable. I'm tempted to buy one of those pay-as-you-go things, but my mother's frozen my bank account. I'm penniless.

One more night.

I check my watch. Liz's party is just getting started. I doubt Anne will even show. Or, when she realizes that I'm not coming, that I'm stuck at home for yet another night, she'll leave.

I tug at my tie and shake the knot loose, unbutton my collar. Kicking off my shoes, I flop down on the bed and glare at my cell. What the hell is happening at that party?

I stare up at the constellation of glow-in-the-dark stars above my bed and pinpoint the big dipper, counting the dots to pass time. They're the only unorthodox accent to a room so typical, it's boring. So boring it's fucking lame.

My cell phone chimes. I glance at the text, knowing it's not Anne, and pause before opening John's message. *She just got here. Looking good.*

I toss the phone on the bed, pretend he hasn't irked me,

that I'm not picturing what she's wearing. With a sigh, I snatch back the cell and type: *Send a picture.*

Seconds later, Anne's face swims onto my screen and instant desire sets my body aflame. Leather pants hug her hips. The black tank underneath her sheer shirt covers just enough skin. Christ, I'm an idiot for asking him to send me a picture. I zoom in on her face. Fuck me. Black liner circles her eyes, and I'm trapped, sucked right in.

I've got to get out of here. But there's no easy way to escape, not without my mother catching me. I've only just earned back some of her trust—break it again, and I'm done.

The soft knock at the door pulls my focus. I click the image closed, turn the ringer to silent, and tuck the phone under my pillow. My mother inches open the door and peers inside. Her expression is hopeful.

"Fixed you a snack."

I choke. "You actually cooked something?"

She steps in a bit farther, silver tray in her hand, and tilts her head to one side. "Well, no, but I carried it myself. That counts for something, right?"

I slide upright so my back presses against the headboard and draw up my legs to make room at the end of the bed. A silent invitation. "Depends what's on the tray."

Taking this as permission, my mother sits on the edge of the mattress. This is a first step, an olive branch, but we're a long way from normal. I've screwed up, caused important people to raise their collective brows. It's her job to bring them back on our side and make them understand I'm young, that it's natural for me to act out. Jesus, what do they expect?

"BLT," she says. "Extra B."

A family favorite—typical Tudor comfort food. And not a bad ploy if my stomach wasn't doing backflips. My cell buzzes from under the pillow, so softly I'm sure only I can hear it. But knowing I have a text inspires me to keep the peace, get my mother out of the room faster, with less drama.

I lean in and sniff the sandwich. "Smells like turkey bacon."

She shrugs. "That's all we had."

"Dad would never have settled for this," I say with a half smile.

At the mention of him, we both go quiet.

"Your father knew which battles to fight," she says, and lifts half the sandwich, takes a bite. Her jaw stretches and flexes until at last, she swallows. "After your performance at dinner, I anticipate a call from Harvard any day. You did well. But this is only the beginning. You know that, right?" She doesn't wait for my answer. "What are you fighting for?"

Freedom.

The opportunity to be myself. To not live under my brother's shadow or be guided by my Dad's final wishes.

Anne.

Another vibration. Another text. "Not everything has to be a war," I say.

My mother stands and walks to the window, gazes out over the lake.

"Your father was just like you when he was young," she says. I open my mouth to protest but no words come out. "I know you think you're so different." She walks across the carpet, pauses at the photograph of me and Arthur, hands behind her back. "You may not believe this, but your dad was wild when I met him. Rebellious."

I try to picture him this way, but can't get past his stoic posture, the permanent stern expression on his face. I can't even recall the craziest thing I've ever seen him do. The realization saddens me.

"He drove too fast, drank too much. Fancied himself a real painter." She turns around and her expression softens. "Maybe you've noticed his obsession with art."

The Pollock at the top of the staircase.

Van Gogh in the dining area. Monet in the master suite.

Our annual charity art gala.

"Did he have talent?" I say.

My mother perches on the edge of my rolltop desk, knocking my marble paperweight onto its side. She picks it up and rests it in the palm of her hand. Rolls it back and forth. "In time, he could have been good, I suppose." With care, she sets the weight on a stack of papers and folds her arms across her chest. "But your father was smart enough to know painting wasn't going to cut it."

She spreads her arms wide, as if to encompass everything in my room. The expensive furniture, the opportunities afforded to me, even the medals on the wall and trophies in the case. Without privilege, I might never have entered Medina Academy. "His art wouldn't have supported us, couldn't have provided all of this . . ."

But what good is *all of this* if you don't have anyone to share it with? The question lingers on my lips. Instead, I say, "It's just stuff."

"That's true." My mother nods. "So, what do you want, Henry?"

Before Arthur died I was quite happy to live spur of the moment, carefree, even careless. My father's last will and testament didn't just shackle me to a future I wasn't sure I wanted, it snuffed out any hope I had of breaking free from all of this. Tonight, though, I wonder if I'd be so resistant to it all if it wasn't shoved down my throat. If I'd made the choices myself.

"I don't know anymore," I say, which is only partially a lie. I want to make my own choices, follow my own path. Explore theater and the arts. Maybe I'm destined for politics—but it's so hard to tell when there doesn't seem to be a choice. But more than all of it, I want Anne.

As if reading my mind, my mother says, "I know you're upset with me about her." A brief pause and then, "But I'm looking out for you. I just don't think she's the right girl." She taps her stomach. "My gut tells me she isn't."

"It's not your gut that matters," I say, though my mouth is dry.

"I know that too," she says. Through her veil of disapproval, the tough exterior she's worked so hard to keep strong, I see into her core and catch a glimmer of the mother I once knew. "But consider this, Henry. If you don't follow this path, become the politician—the man—your father wanted you to become, what kind of life can you offer any woman, let alone Anne?"

She stops to kiss the top of my head before leaving me alone with my thoughts. I consider her words, how far she's come, how far *we've* traveled in just this one talk.

In time, maybe my mother can even accept Anne. At least there's hope.

Another buzz cuts through the silence of the room and I reach under my pillow, grab my phone, anxious and eager, filled with the belief that I can have it all if I want it, if I'm careful. Not just Anne, but all of this, too. I can fulfill my father's expectations, secure my mother's dreams, give Anne whatever she needs. The life she deserves.

The first text causes a lump in my throat.

By the second, that lump is in my chest.

I can hardly stand to look at Catherine's third message. My eyes blur, my pulse races. Adrenaline pumps through my blood, hard and fast. I fling my cell across the room and it smashes against the wall.

I flip open my notebook. My hand tremors as I enter one last lie.

Love conquers all.

CHAPTER TWENTY-EIGHT

Anne

S mile pretty," Marie says before I can even shrug out of
my coat and take in my surroundings.

The steady *thump-thump-thump* of a heavy bass
riff keeps time with the overwhelming trill of squealing,
laughing, chatting, and singing. People emerge from behind
every corner, like snakes slithering out from under rocks.

Liz's home is the poor cousin to Catherine's or Henry's.
Not enough glitter, not enough white. The light blue and tan
color scheme gives the illusion of a beach setting, as though
compensating for its lack of a lakeside view. The kitchen
buzzes with animated chatter on my left, there's dancing
to my right, and then there's Marie, her smartphone camera
aimed right at my face.

"What kind of smile is that?" she says with a sad shake of
her head. Loose curls swing left and right. "This is for Henry.
Let's see some sass."

My throat goes dry. "He's not coming?"

Marie rolls her eyes with exaggeration. "He'll be here." She snaps another picture. "I just want to give him a little incentive to hurry up."

I pose again, this time with my hands on my hips, chest pushed out a little. It's awkward and uncomfortable, but it's for Henry. And the way Marie "oohs" and "ahhs" with each tilt of my head makes me feel pretty, almost sexy, like a model.

"That will get his adrenaline pumping," she says.

I rub my hands together and look around, not sure where to go, what to do, whether I even belong. I held off on arriving until the last minute, hoping Henry would already be here. But it's clear the party's in full swing, and those not on the dance floor slug back drinks. Maybe that's what I need.

The music switches songs and everyone on the make-shift dance floor disperses. Liz emerges from the crowd and slinks over. The V-cut of her shirt is so low you can almost see her ribs.

"What's your poison?" she asks, a little out of breath. A sheen of sweat covers her forehead and neck. "I've got a little beer and a lot of vodka."

I consider the options. Thomas dropped me off, but I'll be cabbing home—which means I don't have to worry about overdoing it. Still, the last time I drank vodka didn't end so well.

"Vodka," Liz says, as though I've taken too long to respond.

She's gone before I can stop her; back in a blink, handing me a tumbler filled with ice. "It's light on the Seven-Up."

I take a sip, force myself not to cringe. She's not kidding about "light."

Someone cranks the stereo and another upbeat tune blows through giant speakers. Against the back wall, the shelves are stocked with bottles of various shapes and sizes. It looks more like a nightclub than someone's living room. Empty glasses clutter the tables. Pretzels, nuts, and popcorn spill from various bowls scattered on every available surface.

Liz leans close and links her arm through mine. "Go ahead and make yourself comfortable," she says, raising her voice over the music. "It's not as fancy as Henry's, but there's a game room down the hall. If you're smoking or toking, take it outside."

I sip more vodka and nod with understanding. She dislodges her arm as a boy I don't recognize drags her onto the dance floor. Glancing back, she gives me one of those helpless looks, and before long, their bodies become a blur of motion.

My cell trills with an incoming text from Sam: *U there?*

I respond: *Yes . . . he's not.*

My eyes flit to the front door, willing it to open, for Henry to walk through.

Sam texts: *Something feels off.*

I got this, I reply.

The text offers more confidence than I feel. My nerves bounce around in my stomach at the anticipation of being with Henry again. Even though he insists again and again that we're okay, that he's not mad anymore, doesn't regret covering for me, I sense that maybe things aren't okay, that there's something he isn't saying. He's starting to slip away.

I can't lose him. This is exactly where I need to be.

Sam responds: *I get it—you're tough. But watch yourself. I can't protect u.*

I never asked you to.

Annoyed, I stuff my phone into my purse. I'm sick of the warnings and advice. Why doesn't she understand that I'm doing what I have to, whatever it takes to show Henry I can be who he needs me to be?

"You know the saying, right?" says a slimy voice from behind me. My back goes rigid.

I turn slowly to face John. Maybe I'm willing to make an effort with Catherine and her lemmings, but Henry can't expect me to be okay with John. I gulp down the rest of my drink. John's taint doesn't go away, sticks to the roof of my mouth. "I give up."

John smirks. "A watched door never opens."

I move to sidestep around him, but I'm stopped by Catherine—her phone is aimed at me, as if she's the self-appointed paparazzi. "Smile, you two," she says. And before I can protest, escape from being photographed with John—of all people, *John!*—the flash blinks in my eye, blinding in the otherwise dim light.

I haven't even recovered when Liz slides in and replaces my empty tumbler with a new full glass. "A little more Seven-Up this round. I may have made that last drink a bit strong," she says, before leaving me alone with my glass.

I'm surprised at how easy this is, how for the first time I don't feel as if anyone is judging me or shaming me. Maybe if I just try a little harder, I'll really fit in, become part of this group. If not for me, then for Henry.

It's always about Henry.

A squeal from the kitchen draws my attention. I spin around to see Catherine, Marie, and Liz now crowding around the counter, their wrists lying upright on the marble surface. John squeezes lime onto their skin, sprinkles it with salt, and then hands them each a shot glass.

Tequila. My stomach roils a bit at the thought. Even with lime and salt, that shit is nasty.

I turn away, nervous I'll get called into action. Immediately, my body collides with a broad chest now covered with my vodka and Seven. "Fuck," I say, eyes locked on the wet splotch spreading across his shirt. "I'm sorry."

"You're not forgiven."

My head snaps up and I connect with the most sparkling pair of blue eyes I've ever seen. He's not exactly handsome, but there's something friendly about his face.

I pause, study the material of his shirt. Not quite a sweater, too thick to be a T-shirt. "Want me to pay for dry cleaning?"

"How about a dance instead?" he says.

I hesitate, glance around, and wonder about Henry, about what's taking him so long, what he'll think if he comes in and sees me dancing with this stranger. But the dance floor fills with couples and not only couples, girls with girls and boys randomly throwing their arms around. It's just one dance.

"Why not," I say, and like magic, Liz is beside me again to remove the now empty glass from my hand.

"Have fun," she says, a slight slur in her voice.

Tequila, I think. That stuff is bad-bad-*bad*.

"Geoffrey," the guy says as we ease onto the floor and bump elbows with thrashers. "I'm from across the bridge. Seattle."

My stomach knots into a big, roiling mass like a bucket of eels. Medina is secluded, tucked away from the bright lights and skyscrapers. A million miles from my past. I focus on dancing, on not making a fool of myself. My head feels a little spinny, but I'm sure it's from the overpowering scent of cologne and perfume mingling and mixing, sending tingles to my temples, making me dizzy. "I'm Anne," I say.

"You're beautiful," he shouts.

Warmth creeps up my neck.

"And you're cute when you blush," he adds.

As I tilt my head back to laugh, I catch Catherine's silhouette in my periphery. She snaps another picture and gives me a thumbs-up.

"Excuse me," I say to Geoffrey, and run after her. As I catch up, she's just finishing a text and a balloon of dread swells in my chest.

"Did you send Henry that picture?" I say. The question snaps out and I try to grab it back, sound less defensive. *We were just dancing, not even touching*, I want to clarify, even though it sounds ridiculous.

Catherine shows me her phone and I read the message: *See, Anne is having fun. Told you we would all make an effort.*

I chew on my lower lip, hoping he'll message back. "Is he coming?"

Catherine grabs her phone. "Very soon," she says, and glances down at my empty hand. "But you need more booze, hon."

"I'll hold off for Henry."

"Nonsense," she says. She tugs on my hand and drags me to the kitchen. "Look, I know we got off to a rough start. I'd like it if we could start fresh."

I'm not even sure what to say to that, so I let it go.

Marie and Liz are doing tequila shots again, or maybe they never stopped. A half-empty bottle sits on the counter surrounded by a sea of squeezed lime wedges. When the girls see me, their eyes light up.

"Anne! Do shots with us!"

I shake my head no, but a drunken Liz grabs my wrist and slams it on the counter with enough force that I wince.

She leans onto my arm, looks up at me, and giggles. Her curly hair fans out in front of her eyes. The scent of alcohol leaches from her skin. She's so wasted I feel sorry for her. "Shit, did I hurt you?" she says, and gasps. "Wait! I can make it better."

She squeezes a wedge of lime and a seed shoots up and hits me in the face. I yank my arm away, a little pissed.

"Here, let me help," comes a deep voice from behind.

My stomach drops to the ground and I want to walk away, to just leave, but Henry will be here soon, Catherine keeps saying, and no matter how big Liz's house is, there's no way to avoid John.

He takes my wrist in his hand. I don't pull away despite my better judgement. He squeezes some lime onto my skin, follows it up with salt. Our eyes meet when he hands me the shot glass and a dangerous spark zips along my spine. He's daring me to drink. To keep up. To fit in.

And even though I know better, know without question that this is a terrible horrible stupid mistake, I lick my wrist, down the shot, and slam the glass on the counter. A shudder makes my whole body tremble. It tastes horrible, burns my throat. And yet I say nothing when John pours another shot, and another.

"That's enough, John," Catherine says, snatching the fourth, maybe fifth glass from my hand. I swirl my tongue across flesh that is red and raw. Camera flashes blink and click in my side vision and I sway a little. The room is fuzzy. My balance is off. I teeter and grip the countertop for support.

"When is Henry coming?" I slur to anyone who will listen.

"Soon," Marie promises.

"Any minute," Catherine adds.

The room spins. I want to sit, lie down, clear my head. But then the music kicks in, and before I can stop him, John drags me toward the dance floor. We're spinning and laughing, and somehow I have a drink in my hand. I suck it back, start to sing. All around me, people are hooting and whistling.

I'm having fun, so much fun that it's okay I'm dancing with John, drinking with Catherine and her friends, because when Henry gets here, he'll be proud that I'm part of the group now, that I'm working so hard to fit in. He doesn't have to pick sides.

I study John's profile, the grin on his face.

Could I have been wrong about him?

To my left, Liz dances on a table as if she's some kind of stripper. Her hands rub against her hips, slide up and down her sides. There's a crowd of people watching, catcalling, hooting and hollering. I join in with a whistle.

Now Catherine's on the table. She reaches down and yanks Marie up, and all three are giggling and writhing against one another. They're mesmerizing.

The table is full, but I want up there too. I stagger forward and the girls help me, and now all four of us are dancing and giggling, showing off. John reaches up and presses another drink into my hand. Alcohol spills from the glass, drips onto the table, the floor, but no one notices, and I'm having such a good time I don't even realize I'm suddenly dancing all alone.

Surrounded by a circle of cheerleaders. They're whistling, egging me on. My body weaves to the beat, my hips sway slow and seductive. And with every movement, the cheering grows louder. I get caught up in the music, really put on a show. One of my hands rubs my body, my hips, my stomach, my chest—while the other pours vodka into my mouth. I can't even taste the Seven-Up anymore. Pure alcohol burns my throat. But it's okay because they like me. I can sense it, their growing acceptance, and I wait for Henry to get here and see how I'm trying. How I really can fit in.

I stumble, regain balance.

Glance down at my adoring fans.

Catherine and Liz sway together, arms around each other's shoulders, smiling at me from behind their phone cameras. The overhead lights blink, flash, pulse with color like a disco ball.

I toss aside my now-empty glass and give my body a sexy little shake. Really swing my hips. The heel of my boot catches on the edge of the table. I lose my footing, stagger forward. My ankle twists and I begin to fall.

The room spins in slow motion.

I'm sure I'll hit the ground, knock myself out cold, maybe shatter my whole skull, but then—

Strong arms are wrapped around my waist, holding me upright and steady. I blink twice and open my eyes, stare into John's face. One of his hands is on my ass, but I'm too drunk to push it away, too embarrassed to make a scene.

"Thank you," I say with a slur, and crash up against him.

Our noses bump.

Our eyes lock.

John presses his cool lips against mine. I open my mouth to protest. He takes it as permission, an invitation, and jams his tongue into my mouth, the taste of tequila too strong. I try to pull away but my legs are wobbly and his hand grabs tighter, holds me in place. A flash of light streaks my vision.

I turn to witness Catherine's knowing smirk and it all begins to make sense.

Shit.

Her laughter sounds wicked over the music pounding in my head.

No. No. No. This is wrong.

Henry.

My world spins off kilter, lights blare behind my eyes. Bile rises, burning my throat, and I turn away just before my vomit splashes across the hardwood.

CHAPTER TWENTY-NINE
Henry

Mayor Stephen Mandell raises his glass, grins at me from behind the bubbling champagne. "To your future," he says to me, and takes a sip.

"To *our* future," Susan Mandell says. "I have a feeling Henry is going to do great things for all of Washington when his career gets going."

Over the past couple of days, the Tudor mansion has undergone another transformation in anticipation of this dinner—a welcome distraction from the chaos in the rest of my life. Roses replace orchids on the long dining room table. Elegant, but not overbearing, a setting fit for the mayor and his wife. My mother is in prime form this evening. Focused, strategic.

She reaches across the table and wraps her fingers around my wrist, giving the illusion of warmth. We've made amends, but it's only a first step. She doesn't know the real reason

Anne hasn't been around for the past few days—only thinks that she's won.

My mother beams. "The country," she says. "Henry will do great things for this *country*. He is destined for the presidency."

I have a hard time not choking on my champagne.

Mayor Mandell sets his glass on the table and picks up his knife and fork. Hovers his utensils over a plate full of prime rib, seared vegetables, and roasted potatoes. An intimate dinner to celebrate.

Motivate.

I've already messed up my chance at an internship with Catherine's father. I shouldn't be surprised he's shut me out, but the rejection stings. Now that I've convinced my mother I'm back on track, she'll strong-arm the mayor into finding me a position on his team.

This dinner is also my mother's way of keeping me from Anne.

My stomach churns at the thought of her. I've studied the pictures from the party more than a hundred times, thumb poised over the delete button. Anne keeps texting and calling. I don't even know what to say. The images confuse me, incriminate her, piss me the hell off.

I steal a glance at my phone. Another text from John. He's itching to show me the rest of the pictures from the party, the *proof* my friends have collected. No matter how much I want to avoid him—all of them—I promised to hear them out.

Susan Mandell unfolds her napkin and sets it on her lap. "I understand there's a new young lady in your life, Henry," she says.

Across the table, my mother's face reddens and her eyes narrow to slits. While I've done what she's asked, followed every damn rule, the subject of Anne is still off-limits in this house.

"You know, I really liked Catherine," the mayor says. He cuts his meat, inspects the color, and shoves it into his mouth. "You two were good together. What happened there?"

I glance to my mother for help, for some indication of how she wants this conversation to go. Somehow, I doubt honesty is the best policy. I take a bite of potato to buy me some time, relieved when the mayor's wife cuts in.

"Oh, Stephen, don't go badgering the boy. They're just kids. I'm sure Henry had good reason for breaking things off." She tilts her head a little and one of her diamond earrings sparkles under the overhead chandelier. "You're dating the Boleyn girl, right?"

I nod, still a little nervous. "Anne and I are seeing each other," I finally say. The words catch in my throat. Such a simple explanation for something so . . . complex.

"Her stepfather is quite the talent," Stephen says, launching into a detailed description of the architectural projects on Thomas Harris's work list. Beyond the theater, he's in charge of redesigning half of downtown, including City Hall. "Our new council offices will overlook the lake."

"Won't that be nice," my mother says with forced enthusiasm. I recognize the gesture as a way to change the topic off Anne—and for once I'm not opposed. I've done everything I can not to think about Anne.

But the Mandells aren't picking up on the clues.

"Dating the architect's stepdaughter will certainly give you some clout," the mayor says. "But an internship with Catherine's father would have given your career the real boost. It's a competitive world out there."

"With that in mind, what do you have planned for Henry?" my mother says, a skilled interception. "I'm positive you'll find a position that fits."

The sing-song echo of the doorbell interrupts his response. I stand, but my mother motions for me to remain seated. "The butler will get it," she says. "There's no need to interrupt dinner."

The bell chimes again, and then immediately a third time, like whoever's on the other side is desperate or frantic to get inside. I shift, once again trying to stand. My mother stops me with a pointed look and I settle into my chair. A wave of foreboding washes over me, and then—

The foyer erupts with voices that rise with increasing intensity—one female, the other our butler. The air around us balloons with tension. But it's impossible not to hear what's going on.

The female voice rises to a hysterical scream, bouncing

off the walls and echoing throughout the whole main floor.

There's a loud crash.

A bellowed, "Stop. You cannot go in there!"

And then, the distinct thump of heavy footsteps across the hardwood floor.

I know it's Anne before she even crosses the threshold of the dining area. Her nostrils flare. Wet streaks trail from her eyes to her chin. Her mascara is smeared, giving her giant raccoon eyes that seem more gothic than alluring. Matted chunks of hair stick to her forehead, the side of her face, along her neck.

My stomach flips. She's an emotional train wreck, but fuck she's a beautiful disaster.

"Henry, why haven't you answered my texts?" she says, oblivious to the room, to the shock on my mother's face. "I can explain. . . ."

Pushing back my chair, I stand, open my mouth to say something—but no words come out. My whole body fills with humiliation. For me. For Anne. For all of this.

The mayor's wife covers her mouth. There's barely a sound, like she's gasping for breath, or hiccupping.

"Anne," I say, and almost trip over my chair in an effort to get to her, to escort her out before she makes things worse. "This isn't the time."

Her wild eyes darken, turn almost matte. Anne backs away, holding her hands upright, like she's fending off some beast. "Shit, fuck, shit. I'm sorry." She shakes her head. Bursts into tears. "I'll leave," she says, already starting for the door.

She glances back at my mother, the mayor and his wife. Mrs. Mandell's jaw is slack, her eyes wide and sympathetic. "I'm sorry," Anne says. "I'm so, so sorry."

I chase after her, deflecting the low whispers at my back. My mother making excuses, Mrs. Mandell assuring her everything will be okay, the mayor tsking, questioning my decisions, my choices. When I catch up to Anne, she stands at the open door looking helpless and lost.

Her motorcycle lies on my front lawn, her helmet on the sidewalk, leather coat strewn across the front step. It's like she half-stripped when she got to the house.

"We can't do this now," I say, wincing as her face falls with understanding. "This dinner is important."

Her voice is barely a whisper. "Aren't we . . . important?"

Pain wraps around my heart, squeezes so hard I gasp. I don't have the words to make this okay. The more entrenched I become in the life that is expected of me, the more I wonder if my friends and family aren't right—maybe Anne really doesn't belong.

"Look, I know those pictures look bad," she says. "It's not what you think." She takes a step toward me, but I back away. "I was drinking. They forced . . ."

"Go home, Anne," I say. My voice is so soft I barely recognize myself. "We'll talk tomorrow."

She nods, begins to leave. But at the base of the steps, she turns back, her bottom lip trembling, eyes welling with tears. "I love you, Henry."

"I know," I say—holding back the rest. I love her too. But as I close the massive door on her retreating form, I realize that I want—need—more.

I pause at the dining room, take a second to gather my thoughts, and walk with my head high, shoulders straight, trying my best minimize the impact of what's happened. I prepare for the questions and accusations, my mother's wrath. But if I'm to have a career in politics, I'll have to get used to scandal.

"Is everything all right?" Mrs. Mandell says.

My voice cracks a little. "It will be."

"So . . . the Boleyn girl," the mayor says, stuffing another forkful of prime rib into his mouth. The room falls silent as he chews, swallows, washes it down with another swig of champagne. "You know, I really liked Catherine," he says, thoughtful, with almost eerie nonchalance. "Now there's a girl destined for greatness. The kind of woman you want on your arm as your First Lady."

He doesn't need to finish the thought for me to know what he thinks of Anne.

CHAPTER THIRTY

Anne

Henry's words whisper in the wind: *Go home, Anne.* Through blinding tears I search for it. Not my stepfather's mansion on the lake, not the wretched trailer park of my past, but a place I feel welcome. Safe.

All I feel now is the hollow ache of loss.

A blur of trees bleeds into a long stretch of ivory sand and ebony water, shit I've taken for granted, haven't begun to enjoy. The moon makes the water shimmer, and the beach looks smooth and untouched. Like polished glass.

I'm drawn back to the memory of my introduction to Medina, tucked safely into Henry's Audi, experiencing school, life—*love*—for the first time.

I'm kidnapping you, he'd said, and I'd smiled. *Taking you to my serial killer cabin in the woods.*

I steer Clarice toward Medina Academy, hit the straight-away and twist the throttle. Cold air whips across my fore-

head, stings my eyes, slaps my cheeks. I can't handle the suffocating claustrophobia of my helmet, the constraints of my
leather jacket.

Trapped by the insurmountable sense of dread, about me
and Henry, about . . . us.

There *is* no more us.

By morning, Henry's mother will have told everyone
about how I showed up at her home, intrusive and feral. Desperate. How I've proven yet again that I don't fit in here.

As I close in on Medina Academy, more memories rush
through my mind like a montage of the good, the bad, and
the best. My sister's ex-boyfriend, ex-landlord, ex-life trans-
forming me into some kind of disillusioned princess waiting
for a dragon slayer to save me, to set me free.

I almost had it. That fairy tale ending. My own Prince
Charming.

Henry.

Now, no one is coming to rescue me. Even Sam is ignoring my phone calls and texts—I've lost my two best friends.

I hit the gas and speed into the parking lot.

The empty spaces give me room to weave between the
concrete curbs, leaning my body as far as it will go, right,
then left, taunting, teasing. I navigate the makeshift obstacle
course with precision, speeding up on the curve, braking
before I fall, memorizing every nuance of the road until I
could drive it with my eyes shut.

Clarice's engine sputters, threatening to cut out. I've pieced her back together as best I can, but she's not whole. Parts of her are missing, lost in the accident, or maybe before—

My chest numbs, as though my heart has swollen and enlarged, pushing against the nerves, trying to snuff out my stubborn, stupid, hopeless feelings. I know it doesn't work like that, but it hurts, hurts so bad I'm blinded by the pain.

Get it together.

I pull up to the curb and cut the engine. Lean my bike up against the cobbled sidewalk leading to the ominous front doors. I was scared of them once—now I'd give anything to walk through them, to be united with Henry.

Go home, Anne.

I stare up at the giant fortress of stone walls, the jagged edges of the brick twin towers, and imagine scaling them to the other side. If only I could curl up on one of the long benches in the courtyard, draw comfort from the fountain or the scent of autumn flowers. Take a walk down memory lane, holding hands with Henry, pausing before class for stolen kisses and—

Empty promises.

And now, I have no choice but to go—

Home.

I climb back on Clarice, hesitate before turning over the engine. My trembling fingers grip the handlebars, twist the bike so it faces the front door. Adrenaline pulses through my veins. I hesitate—and then turn the key. Clarice roars to life. The engine sputters and coughs on idle. I need to punch the gas or she'll die.

The bike lunges forward and I brake hard.

The rear wheel lifts off the ground and bounces back onto the sidewalk. My whole body reverberates from the shock. And my nose is practically pressed up against the front door of the school. So close I could touch it.

I turn Clarice, my back, my heart away from Medina Academy. Rev the engine so hard, the rumble is a deafening roar. I twist the handlebar and step on the gas. Loose gravel sprays up from my back tire. I hit a rock, almost skidding out. Desperate to get away.

Tears blur my vision. I gun it out of the parking lot, my headlights carving a path to the exit.

Silhouetted in the distance, Seattle's floating bridge beckons, a lighthouse drawing me away from the school, from Medina, from Henry.

Go home, Anne.

A merciless chuckle escapes my lips.

With Henry, I thought I was home. Suddenly, I have no fucking clue where that is.

CHAPTER THIRTY-ONE

Henry

I yank my coat up around my neck to fend off the cold, half-run from my car to the sidewalk, and duck under the café's green and white awning.

Through the rain-streaked window, I spot round wooden tables, surrounded by oversize leather chairs set on a brown and beige checkerboard floor. At the storefront window, half a dozen recycled glassless window frames dangle from the ceiling, creating some kind of weird mobile. About as abstract as Pollock.

The spicy scent of chai hits me before I even open the door and step inside. Dim lighting and a quietly burning fireplace in the corner give the place a homey feel, warmth, on an otherwise shitty day.

I scan the clusters of customers, look for familiar faces, for Rick and John. No shock I'm the first to arrive. I flop into an empty seat facing the counter and pull out my physics book. Flip to chapter fourteen. I've read it a dozen times, but nothing sticks. The words blur into a faded string of indecipherable characters, jumble around in my head.

"Coffee?"

Her sweet voice pulls my attention, forms a picture of its owner in my mind before I even lift my gaze.

Small round eyes peer through a pair of copper-rimmed glasses. Her light brown hair is swept back into a ponytail, though a few wayward strands fall loose and stick to the side of her pale face. Her skin is so white she's almost a ghost. She holds up a half-full coffeepot and an empty mug, smiles through thin, compressed lips. "Looks like that textbook is getting the best of you. Caffeine works for me."

Weary, I motion for her to pour. "I'm willing to try anything at this point."

Her long, slender fingers tremble as she fills the ceramic mug and then as she reaches into her green apron to pull out a couple of creamers and a packet of sugar.

"I usually like a little coffee with my sugar," I say.

She drops another packet on the table and blushes, says nothing, just waits as I rip them open and pour them into the cup, add two creams, and take a slow sip.

"Not bad," I say with an appraising nod. "Bold, but not overbearing."

"A coffee connoisseur?" she says, and scoops up the garbage. She's average height and build, but there's something that pulls me, keeps me watching, like I can't look away. Maybe it's how different she seems from—

"I've had a lot of expensive brews in my life," I say, prepared to launch into a conversation about exotic imported beans and the best espresso I ever tasted while on my European adventure two summers back. She doesn't take the bait. "I'm Henry." I extend my hand. "Henry Tudor."

She holds up the coffeepot and a fistful of scrap paper as though indicating why she can't shake hands. "Nice to meet you, Henry Tudor," she says, and—

Leaves.

My jaw goes slack. There's an uncomfortable itch in my throat. I resist the urge to call after her, when the door opens and a chill breeze blows through the café, bringing John and Rick in from the cold. John spots me, waves, and the two wind their way around the tables. Pull out a couple of wooden chairs.

John throws a stack of pictures face down on the table.

My chest tightens.

I stare down at them, hands at my sides, afraid to flip them over, convinced that if I ignore them, they'll simply cease to exist.

Across from me, John waits for my reaction, hands jammed in his pockets, hoodie pulled tight up over his ears, to keep warm or hide, whatever works. "I know it's hard, bro," he says.

At the sound of his voice, I lift my head and our gazes meet. Shadows outline his eyes, dark against the pale sheen of his complexion. Black stubble covers his chin and upper lip. He looks a little less arrogant than usual—though maybe that's just wishful thinking on my part.

"You don't have a fucking clue," I say. My voice trembles a little, betraying false bravado.

Even without looking, I know this is the end of Anne and me. Of Anne.

I've probably studied all of the pictures Catherine sent a dozen or more times, making up excuses, debating camera angles, rationalizing every single flirtatious action. But I know those images don't tell the whole story. There are giant gaping holes. And like a jigsaw puzzle, the missing pieces are on the table in front of me.

I flip over the top photograph.

Anne's mocking smile stares back.

"That was the start of it all," Rick says, like his voice-over narration will somehow soften the blow.

The picture is date-stamped, and I recognize Liz's kitchen in the background. Most of the details are blurry, intentionally out of focus, putting Anne at the center of attention.

Maybe I stare at the picture too long, but a part of me realizes this is the last time I'll see her this way—the sexy, wild, brazen girl I fell for. I haven't even set the photograph aside, moved on to the next, and the pinprick hole in my chest has begun filling with venom. It's been like that for days as I filter through the events of the past few weeks.

I look up, but say nothing. Catherine warned me some of the pictures might implicate John. I shouldn't blame him, though, that it isn't his fault. Maybe that's why I'm stalling, scared to see the betrayal I somehow know is there.

"You should leave," I say, my voice cold and hard.

Rick shakes his head. "He stays. We're not letting you do this alone."

I slide the top image onto the table, flip through the next few. A series of photographs show Anne smiling and mingling with my friends. In one picture, she stands close to John, too close for someone she hates. In another, she is licking her wrist, shot glasses all around. Her eyes are turned downward, lashes almost closed. It's like she's looking right at the camera, staring at—

Me.

Desire sweeps across my skin. No matter how angry, how disgusted and embarrassed, I still want her. Those mesmerizing eyes are tattooed onto my soul. I've lost friends for her, lied for her, disappointed my mother for her—all to believe she looks at me, only me, the way she is in this picture.

I flick it aside.

"She drank a lot of tequila," John says, a little quiet, almost nervous.

I'm only a third of the way through the stack and the

knot in my stomach has already grown to the size of a walnut.

"She doesn't like tequila," I say.

Rick scoots back in his chair, scraping the metal legs across the floor. The noise grates on my nerves. When I look up, my gaze settles on the bar where the waitress pours coffee, adds flavoring, whispers with customers and coworkers. Her lips are so thin they almost disappear, but there's something compelling about them, something that makes me stare a little longer than I should.

She looks up and for a quick second our eyes connect. It happens so fast, blink and you'd miss it.

How much did I miss about Anne?

My mother's advice echoes in my subconscious. I rewind my actions, everything I've done, or not done, in the months since I met Anne. The missed speaking engagements, the deception, standing up for her in front of Catherine, John, and all of my friends.

This isn't me.

No matter how hard it is to live in Arthur's shadow, to live up to my family's expectations, I've never resorted to—

I'm a damn walking cliché.

The king of fools.

I flip to the next image. Anne with some guy I don't know, can't place at school, in Medina. Her head tilts back like it does when I say something funny, when she's joking with me.

The picture's grainy, but I'm positive that guy's hand is on my girlfriend's ass.

A jealous charge surges through my muscles, making me twitch. "Who's this goof?"

John leans across the table for a closer look. "Geoffrey? Joffrey? Fuck. Can't remember."

I add that picture to the one of Anne licking her wrist. Create a small pile on the table. The other photographs are easy to rationalize, to excuse—I know Anne is just trying to be one of us, to really fit in.

She doesn't.

Maybe I've always known, but the hard realization burrows under my skin and hollows out my bones. Her outburst at my dinner only strengthened the nagging doubt that's lingered since the party. I've got to break it off.

Another set of images shows Anne in various poses, most of them without a drink in her hand. It's hard to believe she's drunk. But her arm is draped around Catherine in one, eyes a little too red. I've known Catherine long enough to read the body language—stiff, uncomfortable, looking for an escape. There are two pictures of Anne doing tequila shots. The background is fuzzy. Geoffrey—*Gregory?*—makes an appearance in one of them. Anne is pressed up against him, looking up in adoration as though she's tripped and he's saved her.

"So, she drank too much," I say, trying to ignore the growing lump in my gut. It's twice the size now, two times as heavy. If I stood in the middle of the floor, I'd drop straight through. "People do stupid things when they're drunk."

I shove the stack of remaining pictures aside and lean back, take a sip of cold coffee. The excuse doesn't sit with my friends. Hell, it doesn't even sit with me.

Rick nods, slow, as if he's taking time to form the right words. "For sure," he finally says, and rests his hands on the table to lean forward. "But she's out of control. Look what happened last time she got drunk."

Neither of them knows the real story of the accident, but the rumors are hard to ignore—especially when I know they're true. The waitress walks by again, glances at our table. The surface is peppered with inappropriate photographs—I'm almost embarrassed to know what she's thinking.

I gather them up quickly, but in my rush the bottom picture floats onto the table, image side up.

A sharp pain radiates through my chest.

Two bodies press together, heads angled, lips interlocked. Even without asking, without absolute confirmation, I know that's John's mouth on Anne's, his hand on her ass.

A growl rips through me.

I reach across the table and grab John's collar, yanking him close. Rage explodes through my muscles. My face is so hot I'm sure it will burst into flame. "You bastard."

"Back off, Henry," Rick says, always the mediator, the voice of reason. "He didn't do anything wrong."

"Bullshit," I say. A fleck of spit lands on John's cheek. He doesn't flinch. The back of my neck heats up, and I release John's hoodie, aware we've attracted attention.

"We had a deal," John says, his tone gruff. "She's a tramp. This is proof."

"You set her up."

"No one poured the booze down her throat," Rick says.

I rub my hand across the photograph and close my eyes, remembering a time when Anne danced for me. How my heart raced and my blood boiled. How I would have done anything then, anything she wanted, to make her mine.

A low groan of denial explodes from my lips.

I have sacrificed so much.

My eyes fall back on the photograph. I can't help it. "Looks like you enjoyed yourself," I say to John.

He shrugs. "We were drinking, man. Shit happened." He hangs his head. "Maybe it shouldn't have, but the way she was going . . ." A long sigh, and then, ". . . if it wasn't me, it would have been someone else."

I snarl. "It should have been."

"Maybe," Rick says. He spreads out his palms. "But you and I know this isn't about John. She's dangerous, Henry."

"She'll destroy you," John adds.

I start playing the familiar game of *What if*. What if I'd fought harder, defied my mother and gone to the party? Could I have avoided all of this?

The sharp, stabbing pain in my rib cage betrays the truth. I'm tired of the questions, the assumptions, the complications. I can't live my life with Anne on pins and needles, waiting to get stabbed.

"She's not for you," John says, and points to the pictures. "Even without all of this. She's not right. Your mother will never accept her. None of us will."

No matter how many times I blink, I can't erase the images of Anne dancing, smiling, touching someone else's body. The snapshots play back like a film in slow motion, but the reel stops just before the party, before everything started to go wrong. I'm numb. I can't even remember how it feels to be with her.

"What's the play, man?" John says.

All of this evidence is contrived. But even when I look past it, try to see through to the other side, to *her* side, set up or not, she still *did* those things.

And because of that, I can't navigate the path to a future with her. I know it, my mother knows it, hell, the bloody *mayor* knows it: She doesn't fucking fit.

"With the right mix of pictures, we could have her expelled," Rick says, a little too casual, like he's trying to make it my idea, trying to gauge my consent. I can tell it's something they've talked about—the climax of their plan. I chew on my bottom lip, consider the options, the implications of what they're suggesting.

"No," I say. "It doesn't need to go that far."

The waitress passes our table.

"Huh," John says, catching me staring a little too long. A leer plays on his mouth. "You like that? She looks a little plain to me."

Despite everything, my lips curl into a smirk. "Keep it that way."

Rick reaches across the table, picks up the pictures, and stuffs them in his backpack. "You don't worry about this," he says. "Whatever happens, the key is that you see who she really is, right?"

"Sure," I say, though my mind is jumbled. My heart sore. I can't imagine how to exist with Anne now that I'm no longer under her spell.

As my friends leave, I grab my coffee cup and stand, make my way to the bar.

A few customers wait in line ahead, giving me the opportunity to study the way the waitress works, interacts, smiles. I like how she wipes her hands on her apron after pouring a drink, the way her glasses slide to the bridge of her nose when she's steaming milk.

"You again," she says. There's no edge, no animosity to her voice, just a light teasing that stirs something in my chest, a tingling feeling—of renewed hope.

"How's the caffeine working on that physics homework?"

"Got anything stronger?" I say, and set my cup on the counter.

"Espresso?"

"Only if you make it the way the Italians do," I say, voice low, like we're sharing some dark caffeinated secret. "There's this cute little café in Tuscany. Serves the most perfect espresso . . ."

"Tough to compete with that," she says with a little wink.

I can't tell if she's impressed or indulging me, and decide it almost doesn't matter. I smile.

When she hands me the coffee, our fingers touch a snapshot too long. "What's your name?" I say.

"Jane," she says, and my pulse ratchets up a beat. "Jane Seymour."

"A pleasure to meet you, Miss Seymour," I say, and pump my eyebrows. Twice. "Maybe I'll see you around some time?"

CHAPTER THIRTY-TWO

Anne

Pushpins press into my fingers, feet, and neck, stab the six photographs on the corkboard, each more incriminating and embarrassing than the next. Is this really how it ends?

I sit tall, press my thighs into the hard wooden chair. Scan the room.

Row upon row of bench seating fills with students. The buzzing of gossip vibrates in the room, floating up whispers and accusations and assumptions and lies. At the front, Catherine, Liz, and Marie sit, legs crossed, uniforms pressed, skin properly covered. I find Rick and Thomas near the back, and then there's John.

His dark suit can't mask his smarmy underbelly. He sneers and I shake with disgust. Maybe sensing my discomfort, he winks, kicking my gag reflex up a notch. This whole thing makes me sick.

To my left, the lectern remains empty, the cherrywood handle of the gavel pointed toward me like an omen, as if "court" is already adjourned, judgment passed. As if in the haze of the past week, day, hour, somehow I missed—

The end.

Henry hasn't waited at my locker in days. Hasn't texted. Hasn't called. He hasn't made time for me, for . . . us. Despite his promise to "talk tomorrow"—tomorrow never came. And when the summons from Student Council arrived a few days ago, Henry wasn't there to say everything would be okay.

A dull ache swells in my chest and I blink away a tear.

A commotion at the door pulls my focus to the front of the room.

Henry.

He looks fine on the surface, polished and professional in a charcoal suit, hair slicked back, every strand gelled, stuck, glued into place. Like he's nervous if one comes loose, it will kick-start his unraveling. But beneath that perfect exterior, I can feel his pain.

Maybe that's why he won't look at me, can't meet my gaze.

On his way to the front of the room, he nods at his peers, offering a tight smile to Catherine and his fellow Student Council members. I don't recognize this version of Henry. He is serious. Pulled together.

Foreign.

A regression to the man I first met at the charity gala, a perfect portrait of the Tudor he is destined to become.

The tiny hairs on my arms stand upright.

I finger the necklace Henry gave me.

He takes his position behind the lectern and pauses. Sam approaches to his left, whispers something into his ear, and looks at me over his right shoulder with pity. It's more than I can bear. I've tried to apologize for my abrupt text during the party, even asked for her advice, sought her out in the halls. She's avoided me too. I'm very much on my own.

Henry taps the gavel with a hollow *thwack*. A hush falls over the room.

I'm worried. Even in Henry's profile, I can see the weariness in his eyes, the heaviness in his brow, the stiff set of his shoulders. Whatever act he's putting on for his peers doesn't work on me—*I know him*. He can't fake his feelings with me.

He clears his throat. "On this nineteenth day of December, I hereby call to order the Court of Student Affairs in the matter of Medina Academy versus Boleyn."

A murmur ripples through the crowd.

Henry shifts his body in my direction, but he doesn't look at me—not right at me, anyway. He stares over at the wall and the long line of presidential photographs, the students who are important, have done important things, will make history: Henry's grandfather, father, brother.

Soon another Tudor's picture will hang in the succession.

"Thank you for attending," Henry says.

The low baritone of his voice curls my toes with longing, and I want to melt into him, beg him to stop this before it goes too far. But I won't bow to this makeshift courtroom. "Not like I had much choice."

Henry hesitates and for a moment my pulse quickens. Waits for the spark of hope. But he recovers fast, and when he finally settles his cold gaze on me, my blood hardens like ice.

"Ms. Boleyn, you have been charged with inappropriate conduct, as per section ten, paragraph three of the Code of Conduct written and enforced by the Medina Academy Student Council." Through his suit jacket, his chest contracts like he's swallowed a giant hot-air balloon. "If found guilty, you will face immediate expulsion with no opportunity for a retrial. Do you understand this charge as stated?"

I nod, unable to speak. No one has granted me permission to object, or enter a plea, but I know without question, beyond reasonable doubt, no matter what transpires here, whatever verdict Henry declares, I am already guilty.

Sam stands, clears her throat. "Council calls Geoffrey Spence to the stand."

My eyes flit to the pictures on the corkboard. Geoffrey is Exhibit C.

I almost forget what he looks like until he's halfway up the aisle. Broad chest, thick arms, flat abdominals, like he spends a little too much time at the gym. The scent of body wash sweeps under my nose as he walks in front of me, takes his position, swears to tell the truth and all that BS.

Sam unpins Exhibit C. Holds it up for the room to see, pretending the entire school hasn't seen the pictures, hasn't whispered about them for days. "This is obviously you in the photograph," Sam says, and offers him a sympathetic grimace.

The routine fact check is nothing more than a smoke-screen for what is clearly a witch hunt.

"Can you tell me where you are in this picture?"

Geoffrey nudges his chin toward the front row, at Liz. "House party," he says.

"And do you attend Medina Academy?"

"No. I'm a senior in Seattle. I play football." A slight pause, and then he says, "Tight end."

A collective giggle whispers through the room. Fuck, I hate jocks.

"And what were you doing at the party?"

He turns to me, stares right into my eyes, and delivers a bold-faced lie. "I was invited by Anne Boleyn."

"Bullshit," I say, the denial rocketing from my lips. Maybe I'm going down, but not without a fight.

A collective gasp silences the room.

"This court will not tolerate that kind of language," Henry says, and raps his gavel on the stand—twice.

It's like I don't hear him, blinded with desperation and

rage, motivated by a primal need to defend myself against this shit. "Before the party, I'd never even seen that fucking guy."

"Language, Ms. Boleyn," Sam says, her tone professional and curt. "You will have an opportunity to speak."

She addresses Geoffrey again. "What did you bring to the party?"

He drops his head. "Tequila," he says. "Ms. Boleyn requested it."

What did they do, hire this guy specifically to screw me over? God knows they can all afford it. I scoff loud enough for Henry to turn to me, eyes blazing, lips set to a thin, immobile line.

"This is ridiculous," I snap. "I don't even like tequila. You know that, Henry."

He hammers the gavel against the top of the lectern with a resounding crack. "That's enough. One more outburst and I will hold you in contempt of this court."

My blood boils, threatens to catch on fire and burn down this whole mockery of a courtroom.

Next, council calls Liz to the stand and asks about the nature of the party.

"Get together," she clarifies. "I specifically requested that nobody bring alcohol. A rule Anne clearly didn't respect."

I resist the urge to give Liz the finger. I'm such an idiot to have believed her.

Sam clears her throat. "And why didn't you ask her to leave?"

Liz looks down, like she's gathering her thoughts. She raises her head and turns to me, eyes welling with false tears. "We were all just trying to help Anne fit in. I didn't want to single her out."

"What a freaking actress," I mutter.

Henry's posture stiffens but he doesn't object.

The court hears similar testimony from Marie, who claims happiness rather than excessive drinking inspired the now famous table dance. Ironic how most of the pictures are of my performance, not of the whole group's.

"Things got crowded when Anne joined us," Marie says. "She was out of control—we didn't want anyone to get hurt."

I begin to grow numb. Wyatt, Rick, even Charles each offers up some kind of *evidence* that I've violated the Code of Conduct, not just at this party, but since the day I set foot in Medina. Inappropriate dress. Uniform violations. Misdemeanors they've put up with, allowed to slip, to help me fit in.

I can hardly hear them anymore, their sentences pieced together like Silly String, and looping into the noose I know waits for my neck.

By the time Catherine is called to the stand, I've almost stopped caring. I already know everything she's going to say. Despite Sam's promise, I doubt anything I have to offer will matter in the end.

I watch the clock, listen to the hollow echo of my heart. It beats too fast against the empty cavern in my chest, threatens to kick and punch its way straight through. I imagine it lying on the floor in a pool of my blood, still beating, pulsing, breathing. My head fills with dizzying confusion, is blown up so full that I'm sure with just one tiny pinprick, my brain will pop.

"Anne's manipulations have turned against her," Catherine says. I push back the tears, focus on staying strong, on the second hand of the clock slicing away another minute of my final moments.

At last, Sam calls John to the witness stand and he begins with the party, talking of inappropriate behavior and my excessive drinking.

"You know what they say about tequila," John says with a shrug. "By the end of the night, she was barely dressed."

I look to Henry to defend me—isn't John's comment breaking some kind of rule?

Henry's Adam's apple twitches.

He sits ramrod straight.

"Anne has always been out of control," John says now. It's like he's being interviewed for a documentary, playing up a role, pretending he knows anything about me. He doesn't. None of them do. None except Henry. "We had this experiment in chem class . . ."

Henry shifts and for a moment and I think he might interject.

"She was all over me," John says, shuddering for effect. "When the lights went out, she . . ." He coughs, clears his throat. "Let's just say she's lucky I didn't make a complaint against her for sexual harassment."

"That's a lie," I say, my voice cool. "You've been on my ass since the first day."

John scoffs, but doesn't deny it.

I look to Henry, challenging him to dispute *this* if nothing else. He was *there*. He witnessed me rejecting John at his party. He understands why. I choke back a sob. "Henry?"

He says nothing.

Sam unpins Exhibit E. John's hands are cropped out of the image, but mine are wrapped around his neck. I'm pressing up against him, chest, nose, lips. It's clear I'm all over him—the photograph makes even *me* cringe.

I tamp back self-loathing and disgust, reminding myself I've been set up, that this isn't me. I would never do this. But Henry sits so still, I'm afraid he's not breathing, that I've killed him somehow, that he's dead. Just a shell.

"To repeat," Sam says, holding the photograph in the air, "your testimony is that Ms. Boleyn drank too much tequila at the party, danced provocatively on a table, and when she fell, you attempted to catch her. And that's when she threw herself at you?"

"It wasn't even a party," John says, and runs his hand

through his perfectly placed hair. "Just a friendly barbecue. The rest of us weren't even drinking."

Another lie. I scan the corkboard of strategically placed evidence. There isn't a single photograph of anyone else with a drink. There's no proof Catherine danced on the table, that Liz matched me shot for shot.

My mouth turns to sandpaper and I realize that I'm done. That it was all a set-up from the start.

Sam turns, faces Henry. Maybe I'm imagining it, but it almost looks like she's smiling a little, having fun at my expense. She's supposed to be my friend. Is the whole damn school against me now? The cavern in my chest widens. "I have no further witnesses," she says.

Henry nods. "Thank you." He shifts again, addressing me with a low, pained tone. "Do you have anything you would like to say in your defense at this time, Ms. Boleyn?"

I search his eyes, look for some reason to fight. Even before the verdict, the sense of loss is eating me alive, swallowing me whole. My body trembles, but I've got to try one last time to get through to Henry, to make him see that—

"I'd like to request a recess," I say.

Another murmur ripples through the crowd.

"That is highly unorthodox," he says.

My nostrils flare. "This whole fucking trial is highly unorthodox," I snap. "It's not even real. I'm clearly being set up."

Henry's jaw leaps with anger. "That excuse is starting to sound a bit clichéd," he says, and I see it in his eyes—he's unraveling.

"That's not fair," I say quietly.

Henry nods stiffly. "I'll grant a ten-minute recess."

It's an admission he's lost some control, a half-assed apology, but like hell I'm letting him off the hook. I follow him out of the room, down the hallway, ignoring the stares and glares slicing into my back.

"Henry!"

He freezes at the sound of my voice, turns around so slowly I can tell he doesn't want to face me.

"We can't do this," he says.

The rawness of his voice gives me hope. I walk toward him; he doesn't run. I reach for his arm; he flinches, but doesn't move my hand. "You know this is a set-up," I say. "I'm not innocent, but none of it happened the way they make it sound."

He yanks out of my grip. "Are you fucking kidding me, Anne?" Reaching back, he rubs the nape of his neck. "It's like goddamn déjà vu."

I'm so wound up I could spit. "What is that supposed to mean?"

"Come on," he says. "This isn't the first time you've been in this position. They can't *all* be lying."

"You think *I* am?"

His jaw has that unmistakable stubborn set.

It's like someone is doing backflips in my gut. "Answer me," I shriek, aware I'm moving well past anger and into hysterics. "Do you think I'm lying?"

Henry scrubs his hands over his face. "Christ, Anne. What am I supposed to think?" He slams his fist against the wall.

The last of my hope leaks out in a horrified squeak. My whole body trembles. "You're a coward."

Henry flinches.

"This evidence is bullshit and you know it," I say, now standing on my tiptoes to get right in his face. I can't decide whether to smack him or kiss him. "If you loved me, had any feelings for me at all, you'd admit it."

Henry looks away and I know I've hit a nerve. "Have you ever wondered," he says, much quieter, with more calm, "why this keeps happening? Why you keep getting in these situations?"

I recoil. His attack on my character hurts more than anything. Is the most pain I've ever felt.

"You used to be on my side," I say quietly.

"It's not about sides," he says, taking a deep breath. "Look, I get it. Some of the facts don't add up."

"So defend me—don't sit there and watch me burn," I say. I'm pissed that I'm crying, but I can't stop.

"That's not my job," he says, and runs his hands through his hair, like he doesn't know what else to do with them. All

I want is for him to pull me into his arms. But I know that's not happening. Will probably never happen again.

Maybe I should let up, but I deserve an explanation. "Maybe not in the courtroom . . . but what about us?"

"There can't be an *us*," he says, and my stomach drops to the floor. Drops under the floor. "You're unpredictable. My life can't—won't be able—to handle that." My heartbeat slows. "I don't want to always be worried about you losing control," he says. "What you might do."

He keeps going. "Look, you'll be okay, Anne." His eyes meet mine and even though I know it's futile, I search them for a thread of hope, something to tell me there's still a chance for us. I'd give up Media Academy, my new friends, Clarice—I'd give up all of it for Henry, for another chance. "You're strong— stronger than all of this," he says, but it's like I can't hear him because he's not saying the right words. "You'll learn from this, go on and do great things." He smiles a little, but it's ironic and sad. "Maybe you'll even be an astronaut."

"And you'll what? Go on to be president? Become the man your family expects you to be?" My chest is on fire. It hurts so damn much. I deserve better than this, am worth more than this public break-up. "Is this really what you want?"

His eyes darken in shadow. "It's what I need."

A spasm of pain rips across my chest and I bite back a scream as he walks away.

I make my way down the hall and into the ladies room

and splash water on my face. Dry my bloodshot and swollen eyes. I lift my chin and head back into the courtroom—deflecting the stares and the slurs, the way John sneers and Catherine scowls. Now I know it's over, there's nothing left.

Henry resumes his position at the podium, coughs, takes a sip of water and sets the crystal glass down. Clears his throat. "I call this session back to order. Is there any further evidence to present?"

A uniformed man steps forward. I've only seen him once. My stomach does a slow roll. Campus security. He whispers something to Henry, hands a small flash drive to Sam. A projector screen rolls down from the ceiling.

Fear catches in my throat even as the first picture of Clarice emerges on the screen. My last act of rebellion, captured on film. Frozen, I watch as my bike crawls into the Medina Academy parking lot, idles, and paces. The room is silent but for the thunderous roar of Clarice.

The engine revs, and I know what happens next. I twist the throttle, leave behind skid marks and—

Oh my God.

The scene unfolds in slow motion. Clarice's tires spin on the asphalt. Loose gravel flies everywhere. The bike lurches forward, kicking up a rock that sails back, back, back, toward the school and, holy shit, no!

One of the windows cracks.

A collective gasp echoes through the room.

I'm sick with remorse. With the engine revved, my thoughts scattered. I never heard the glass break, and I know I'm done. I've broken every last rule.

The screen fades to black.

Voices carry and rise.

Henry slams the gavel on the lectern, and the room goes so still I am terrified to breathe. He turns to me and says, "Is there anything you would like to add, Ms. Boleyn?"

An apology is worthless, and I'm not about to beg. I shake my head, lower my gaze.

Henry clears his throat. "In light of the fact that you've offered no evidence to counter these accusations, I can only pass judgment according to what is presented." His gaze moves to the corkboard and the incriminating photographs. "Based on the testimony heard today, and this video, I find you guilty on multiple counts of inappropriate conduct and damage to school property."

A collective sigh. And then—

"You are hereby expelled from Medina Academy. Effective immediately."

A roar of noise. Some scattered clapping. Henry silences the room with a heavy thud of the gavel.

"Do you wish to say anything at this time?"

My throat is raw, my chest weighs ten million pounds, but I stand and lift my chin. Who cares what they think of me now?

"I get it—I'm guilty. . . ." I pause. "According to your student laws. But you guys know the truth. I was never going to fit in here." I shift my gaze to Catherine. "It's useless to point fingers or shift blame to anyone in this room. I can't dispute those pictures. Well played."

A dull ache swells against my chest and presses against my heart. I draw strength from the pain. I refuse to walk out of here with my tail between my legs. They don't deserve that kind of satisfaction.

"But I hope that each of you"—I scan the length of the first row of students, pause at Catherine, and then John—"can live with what you've done. It's not right. Everyone in this room knows it."

Finally, I turn to Henry, begging my voice not to crack. "You are a good president, Henry. As good as your brother. Better even."

His jaw twitches, and he finally looks up, meets my eyes.

Maybe I'm not good for him. Maybe I can't fit into the perfect life everyone has built for him. But as we stare into each other's eyes, I know that whatever we had was real. It meant something to him, meant something to *me*. "You'll do the right thing in the future—really make a difference." I blink against the tears threatening to fall. "I have to believe that. Because it's the only way I can accept this."

Whispers echo through the crowd.

I search his face for a sign that he understands the message, that it's not the party I regret, not the falsified mistakes I've made, not even breaking the rules, but that I couldn't be who he needed, that I embarrassed him, embarrassed myself.

Henry offers only a stiff nod, then taps the gavel one last time. "I hereby deem this session adjourned."

The room falls silent, and I wonder how long I'll hear that gavel echo through my dreams.

Henry gathers his papers and stuffs them into a file folder. Smoothes out the creases in his pants. For one dizzying moment of bitterness and hope, I worry that he will turn to me, say something final, say anything at all.

My breath catches in my throat.

Students file out of the room, hushed voices rising as they hit the hallway. By tomorrow, they will have forgotten this, forgotten—

Me.

But I will never forget

When the last student leaves, Henry stands at the corkboard, carefully removing the pins from Exhibit B, C, D, and F.

Look back. Please look back.

He pulls the pin on Exhibit E.

My chest swells so fast I think it will burst. I make my eyes go wide, so big they're like saucers, but the tears won't stop.

Henry stares at the last exhibit. Shoulders rigid. I know without looking what's on the print. The first photograph of the evening, the picture that started it all. Marie's voice echoes in my memory: *It's for Henry. Give me some sass.*

I chew on my lower lip so hard I draw blood. Its coppery taint pools under my tongue.

Look back, I beg in silence. *Just look at me one more time.*

But Henry doesn't turn. His shoulders slump. One

two

three seconds pass.

I love you.

The pushpin holding up the last picture is stuck in my throat. Henry grabs the corner and yanks. The bottom half of the image rips and floats to the floor.

The door clicks shut behind him and he's gone.

I gather my belongings, suddenly desperate, ready to leave this place, these people, leave Henry behind. With my hand on the door handle, I pause at what's left of the exhibits, my heart heavy and broken.

But all that remains is the stark image of my severed head.

ACKNOWLEDGMENTS

It's cliché but true that it takes a village to raise a child, and that is perhaps no more relevant for me than with the "birth" of *Anne & Henry*. From its earliest origins, this book has enjoyed the support and encouragement of some incredibly supportive people, beginning with my amazing agent Mandy Hubbard and the awesome Bree Ogden (a true Tudor expert and Anne Boleyn fan).

Sometimes, when I'm having a (stereo)typical writerly doubt kind of day, I look back on those e-mails where Mandy and Bree fed my fragile ego with inspiration and unwavering praise. Thank you ladies for your (ginormous) part in making this publishing dream come true. Your passion for this book and for my portrayal of the characters means more to me than I could ever acknowledge in words.

As I write this, thinking of all the words she'd probably strike through, I struggle not to make this acknowledgement page "An Ode to Sara Sargent." As an editor, Sara is professional, thorough, and brilliant, if not at times a royal pain in the ass—what the heck is wrong with breathing, inhaling, exhaling, smirking, laughing, and smiling, anyway? In all seriousness, this book is so much more for her insight, skill, and absolute faith. From her earliest revision notes, peppered with hand-drawn hearts and stars, to her (almost) daily e-mails that made me laugh and cry (I know you're not surprised, hon!), she's become so much more than an editor. Sara, I can never thank you enough for all that you've taught me, and the support you—and the entire Simon Pulse team—has given to me and this book. Thank you for believing in me.

A giant virtual hug to Regina Flath, who designed a dream cover for *Anne & Henry*. Thank you for "getting" this story. I could not have envisioned a more perfect cover. You are brilliant.

Eternal gratitude to my writing mentors Gary Braver, Steve Berry, James Rollins, and Jacquelyn Mitchard, who taught me to write tight, write often, and to always dream big.

Writing is, by nature, a solitary act, but I am so fortunate to be surrounded by friends and family who have acted as cheerleaders for not only this book, but also my entire career. To my remarkable critique partners Kyle Kerr, Kitty Keswick, and Rocky Hatley, my undying gratitude for reading, rereading, and rereading Anne & Henry yet again, for listening to me whine, and for (repeatedly) picking me up when I thought I was down for the count. I know you can recite this book word for word by now—and yet, there are not enough words to thank you.

And to my awesome beta readers Karen Dyck (my Henry VIII expert!); Bessie McLaughlin (thrilled you love THIS version of Henry); Savannah and Amanda Ius (write your books, ladies); James Grasdal (chief cheerleader); Brandon Freund (thanks for American Politics 101, now finish writing your book!); and Hailey Pelletier—your feedback, knowledge, and keen reading skills are, as always, invaluable. Special thanks to my early chapter readers Jessica Bell, Karen Bass, Louise Gorenall, and Jamie Provencal, and to my always-there pom-pom waver, Sue Worobetz. You've talked me down from many a cliff—thank you.

To my incredible sister, Jessica Driscoll—you are my rock. There is nothing I could say that could ever adequately convey how much I love and appreciate all that you have done, and continue to do for me, not only for this book, but Every. Single. Day. I love you so very much.

I am incredibly fortunate to have such support from my entire family. Thank you, Dad, for buying me that old rolltop desk, begrudgingly admitting that you supported my career choice, even if it meant I'd always be a "starving artist" and you wouldn't be able to retire—ever. And to my mom, for encouraging me to be Alice (your dreamer)—even if this book isn't a Lee Child–like story. (Hey, there're no vampires!)

And to my amazing stepfather, Simon Angell, whose love of me, coupled with his love for Anne Boleyn, made writing this book that much more important.

Last—but certainly not least—I thank my beautiful step-daughter, Aydra Dalton, whose words of support can melt the most stubborn self-doubt, and my husband, Jeffrey. You may not fully understand this industry, babe, but you understand me. I love you. Always.

CPSIA information can be obtained at www.ICGtesting.com
Printed in the USA
BVOW021654110412

287452BV00002B/8/P